"You're a lot smarter than you look."

"Why, thank you, ma'am," he replied.

"I mainly just wanted to grab the mail," she said, walking toward the front door, where a few envelopes had been pushed in through the narrow slot and were piled on the floor.

Leon had locked the back door behind him and was heading into the main office when he heard the sound of shattering glass.

He raced forward and saw a hole in the plate glass window. Then he spotted Cassie, apparently unscathed, looking toward the ground. He was just rounding a desk to reach a point where he'd be able to see what was on the floor when a second object crashed through the window.

The object landed on the floor and rolled to a stop. Metal. Cylindrical. And something attached to the end. Like maybe a detonator.

"Bomb!" he yelled, grabbing Cassie and half dragging, half carrying her as he raced for the back exit. He had to get them both outside before the devices exploded.

But he was too late.

Jenna Night comes from a family of Southern-born natural storytellers. Her parents were avid readers and the house was always filled with books. No wonder she grew up wanting to tell her own stories. She's lived on both coasts but currently resides in the Inland Northwest, where she's astonished by the occasional glimpse of a moose, a herd of elk or a soaring eagle.

Books by Jenna Night

Love Inspired Suspense

Rock Solid Bounty Hunters

Visit the Author Profile page at Harlequin.com.

COLD CASE MANHUNT

JENNA NIGHT

LOVE INSPIRED SUSPENSE
INSPIRATIONAL ROMANCE

LOVE INSPIRED® SUSPENSE

INSPIRATIONAL ROMANCE

ISBN-13: 978-1-335-55445-1

Recycling programs
for this product may
not exist in your area.

Cold Case Manhunt

This edition published by arrangement with Harlequin Books S.A.

For questions and comments about the quality of this book, please contact us at CustomerService@Harlequin.com.

Love Inspired
22 Adelaide St. West, 40th Floor
Toronto, Ontario M5H 4E3, Canada
www.Harlequin.com

Printed in U.S.A.

Be pleased, O Lord, to deliver me:
O Lord, make haste to help me.
—*Psalm* 40:13

To my mom, Esther. My own North Star.

ONE

Bail bondswoman and bounty hunter Cassie Wheeler had already survived several storms in her life. This late-spring squall, complete with booming thunder, jagged lightning arcing across the night sky and pouring rain was not going to bother her. She wouldn't allow it.

She was driving her SUV along the eastern edge of Lake Bell in Stone River, Idaho, heading for home after spending the last three hours in a courtroom. Bryan Rogan, a former bail-jumping client who'd been recovered by Cassie and her team, had been on trial for selling weapons stolen from a national guard armory.

Rogan was a thirty-year-old man with a string of increasingly violent crimes behind him, and he was known to associate with hardened criminals. The prosecutor had asked Cassie to testify to her interactions with Rogan when she'd apprehended him after he'd jumped bail. How he'd fired several rounds at her and screamed that was going to kill her. The intent of her testimony was to influence the sentence he ended up serving. The man was a danger to society. He needed to be put away for a while.

Cassie had been happy to appear in court, ready to

describe the events in detail. But, as sometimes happened, the court proceedings had not moved along as briskly as scheduled. She would need to go back tomorrow.

Several of Rogan's criminal buddies had sat in the courtroom, glaring at her in an obvious attempt to intimidate her. Cassie had not been impressed.

Her phone rang and she glanced toward the screen in the dashboard. It was Leon Bragg. One of the bounty hunters who worked for her at Rock Solid Bail Bonds.

"What's up?" she asked.

"I just wanted to let you know that I personally saw Rogan get into the transport van," Leon said in his signature deep drawl. "I followed him over to the county jail where the van drove into the sally port and the security door dropped down behind it."

Cassie felt a slight smile lift the corners of her lips. Leon was worried, so he thought *she* must be worried.

"He's on a no-bond hold thanks to his escape attempt. Since I didn't put up a bond for him to appear in court this time, I'm not out any money if Rogan takes off again. Rock Solid Bail Bonds has no financial investment at all in him right now. So stop worrying, *Mom*."

Leon laughed, and the low rumbling sound coming through the speaker in Cassie's SUV had the effect of a warm, relaxing bath, easing all the tense muscles that usually led to a slight headache and neck ache by the end of every working day. In a world gone awry, where so many things were not okay, Leon—who'd had her back more times than she could count—often made her feel like things *could* be okay. Even if just for a short while.

Cassie gave herself a few seconds to enjoy the feeling before she made herself stop. Because Leon was her employee. And she believed in maintaining strong business ethics guidelines, which included a business owner not becoming romantically involved with an employee.

And beyond that, Cassie wasn't someone who should be involved in a romantic relationship, anyway. Her husband, Idaho State Trooper Jake Hollister, had been murdered five years ago. There'd been no known witnesses and minimal physical evidence left behind. The few leads that were developed had quickly turned into dead ends. The investigation had eventually become a cold case.

Cassie thought about her husband's murder several times a day, every single day. More so lately, after getting a hint of information that might be helpful in solving the case. Then again it might not pan out at all. She'd gotten her hopes up only to be disappointed before.

"I know you want to make certain Rogan stays off the streets whether or not you have a financial interest," Leon said, continuing the conversation he'd started. "I think we all feel that way."

"Agreed."

"Okay, I'm heading back to the office," Leon said. "Harry and I both have some files we need to update, and then we'll close everything up for the night."

"Sounds good."

Cassie had hired Harry Orlansky and trained him as a bounty hunter a few months after his wife passed away four years ago. The skills he'd learned in the military, plus his experience as a volunteer with search and rescue alongside Cassie and her dad, had paid off. Harry was a natural. He'd recently gotten remarried. Proof that life did go on after the heartbreaking loss of a spouse. For some people, anyway.

"Man, this rain is really coming down," Leon commented.

"Tell me about it." The downpour had nearly flooded the road Cassie was driving on.

"You almost to the ranch?" he asked.

Cassie rolled her eyes even though he wasn't there to see the gesture. For a guy who made his living hunting down dangerous men—a guy with a past darker than the lives of many of the criminals he now chased—Leon sure could be a worrier.

"I'm just about to the Shackleford Inlet," she said as a flash of lightning illuminated the short bridge ahead. Lake Bell was to the right. The marshy, shallow-water inlet was to the left, with forest just beyond it.

The entrance to North Star Ranch, where she lived with her dad and a husband-and-wife team who helped care for the horses boarded on the property, was only seven miles beyond that.

"Before I forget, Harry wanted me to ask you something," Leon said.

Cassie never heard the question. A bullet ripped through the windshield of her SUV. Two more immediately followed.

"No!" The word flew out of Cassie's mouth as small shards of glass sliced across her face. She tightened her grip on the steering wheel and fought the impulse to turn right or left. She was on the bridge and either direction would take her into the water. If she were knocked unconscious by the impact, which was highly likely, she'd drown before anyone could rescue her. If she slammed on the brakes, she'd be a sitting duck for

the shooter. The bridge was too narrow for her to make a U-turn. Her only option was to drive forward, toward the source of the gunfire. She grit her teeth and hit the accelerator.

"Cassie, tell me what's happening!" Leon barked through the speaker.

"Someone's shooting at me!"

She was aware of hearing his voice again, but his specific words didn't register. At the moment, she had a higher priority than listening to him. She needed to get past the shooter without getting killed.

She flicked a switch beneath the dashboard to dim the instrument panel lights in the hope of making herself a more difficult target, but almost immediately a bolt of lightning flashed overhead, lighting her up like a Broadway theater marquee.

A barrage of bullets tore across the windshield and front of her SUV. The safety glass held together, but the spiderweb of cracks along with the pouring rain made it nearly impossible to see. The SUV slowed and the engine started knocking. A bullet must have made it through the front grill and gotten into the engine.

The disappearance of the reflector buttons on the bridge railings told her she was back on solid ground.

"Cassie!" Leon's voice boomed through the speaker.

"I made it across the bridge," she said while flooring the accelerator, trying to push her damaged vehicle up to at least normal speed so she could get through this ambush—or whatever it was—and make her way home.

She drove into the slight curve just beyond the end of the bridge. At the same time, she heard the loud crack of a rifle shot from just ahead and to her right.

The front driver's-side tire blew out and sent her SUV sliding across the wet road.

"Lord, help!" She offered up that same short prayer repeatedly as she fought with the jerking steering wheel to keep her SUV on the asphalt. She lost the battle. The driver's-side tires went off the pavement into the mud and momentum kept it sliding until the tires sank deeper, got caught in the muck, and the SUV flipped over onto the roof.

One jolt after another rattled her body until all of the various movements finally came to a stop. The air bags had done their job and started to deflate. Cassie, held in place by her seat belt, bit back on the feeling of dizziness and disorientation. She reached to unfasten the clasp and dropped down onto the ceiling. The rollover meant she was now on the side of the vehicle closest to the road. And, presumably, closest to the shooter. She had to move quickly despite the pain in her wrenched neck and shoulders.

The vehicle's electrical system was out. The headlights and interior lights were off. The storm had apparently stalled over Stone River, with lightning still flashing overhead. That could make it easier for the shooter to see her.

Her phone had disconnected from the SUV's hands-free system. She crawled around on the ceiling and found it among a lot of the other stuff that had fallen when the SUV flipped over. She hit the side button to silence it and slid the phone into her pocket. The last thing she needed was to be hiding in the woods and have her phone start making noises.

Cassie made her way to the passenger side and reached down for the door handle out of habit before realizing she needed to reach up. The door only opened an inch or so and then froze. It had been dented. She didn't have time to waste. The shooter was likely closing in, ready to finish her off. She kicked at the door frantically until it finally opened enough for her to slip out.

Just before she did, she reached up for the console between the front seats and pulled the latch. Her gun fell out and she caught it. "Whoever you are, I'm not going to make this easy for you," she muttered, already thinking about the very long list of bail jumpers who held a grudge against her. Maybe this attack was related to her time in court today with Rogan. Maybe it was related to something else entirely.

Her holster was somewhere in the back of the vehicle with her pepper spray, night-vision binoculars and the rest of her bounty hunting gear. She didn't have time to go digging around for it now. Instead, she shoved the gun into the waistband of her pants, pushed out of the SUV into the pouring rain, and immediately found herself ankle-deep in mud.

There was another boom of thunder and flash of lightning overhead and she risked a glance back toward the road. She saw a man standing at the edge of the pavement where her SUV had left the asphalt. He was wearing a ski mask and hat, and had the collar of his jacket turned up. She couldn't see his face. But she could see the rifle in his hands. And she knew that he saw her. Because he'd been turning his head from side to side as if searching for something when she'd first spotted him. Now he locked his face in her direction and lifted the rifle to take aim.

Cassie turned and took off into the woods, trying to

run, but the sludge grasping at her boots made it difficult.

She needed to call 9-1-1. But before she could do that, she had to find a place where she could stay safely hidden until help arrived. Taking a stand and trying to fight back against the gunman in the dark when he could have night-vision equipment and she did not was foolhardy.

She headed deeper into the thick forest, her hair and clothes snagging on pine needles as she shoved her way through the stabbing tree branches. In broad daylight, the clues she was leaving behind would be as obvious as flags marking a hiking trail for an experienced tracker. She could only hope that the lunatic chasing her was not skilled at hunting humans. Or that he was in too much of a hurry to look around.

She was used to hiking in the woods, and jogging on occasion to stay fit, so she made good headway. Given the rocks, exposed tree roots and uneven terrain she was traversing, there was no way she could make a call for help while running. She had to pay attention to her footing. Finally, she reached a point where she thought it might be relatively safe to stop and make that call.

Lightning flashed again. Seconds later, Cassie heard the crack of a rifle shot, followed by booming thunder. Burning pain creased her left arm and she stumbled forward, falling onto her hands and knees. She'd been shot. She felt the gun fall out of her waistband and, for a few frantic seconds, couldn't find it on the forest floor in the darkness.

When she finally did recover it, she decided to hold on to it, safety off and ready to fire, rather than tuck it back into her waistband.

The rain was pattering so loudly on the tree limbs

and on the small expanses of exposed ground that she couldn't hear if the gunman was moving in on her. Without the flashes of lightning, she couldn't see much. But she knew there was a nearby stream that came down from the mountains and emptied into the lake. If she hiked in the bed of the stream, she wouldn't leave a trail. She headed for it, finally stepping into roiling water and fighting to keep her balance on the uneven layer of river stones.

Following it downstream would take her back to the road. The last place she wanted to be. She headed upstream, anxious to move at least a couple hundred yards so she might finally feel it was safe enough to stop for a few seconds to try to make the call again. She also needed to check her gunshot wound. See how bad it was and figure out if she was in even worse trouble than she already knew she was.

"Cassie, *answer your phone!*" Leon Bragg drove his truck full-throttle around Lake Bell toward the bridge over Shackleford Inlet. He knew that yelling in frustration at the ringing sound coming through the speaker would not accomplish anything, but at least it was something he could *do.*

Sixteen minutes ago, he'd heard a popping sound on Cassie's end of the phone, followed by her yelling no, and then a jumble of sounds before the call disconnected. He'd been on his way to the office and had immediately changed direction, heading toward Cassie to see what had happened and to make sure she was okay. He'd tried repeatedly to call since then and had gotten no answer.

The weather was bad. She could have had an accident. Maybe a tire blew out. Or maybe one of the criminals she'd helped put away over the years had tracked her down looking for revenge. A lot of fugitives they recovered made that threat to Cassie. Leon could only think of a couple of times when someone had made that threat to him. They didn't threaten his fellow bounty hunters Harry Orlansky or Martin Silverdeer nearly as often, either. The reason for the difference was obvious. It was because she was a woman and she didn't look particularly intimidating.

Leon knew that despite her smaller stature, Cassie was smart and strong and tough. But she wasn't superhuman. Nobody was. Everyone needed help sometimes, and he would be just as worried and have the exact same reaction if he were on the phone with Harry or Martin and the call ended the same way.

Okay, that was a lie. One that he'd been telling himself for a while. His reaction to the possibility she was in danger *was* different. He'd given in to the impulse to physically check on her more quickly than he would have if it had been one of the guys on the phone with him. That would have been the case if he'd been on the phone with any woman. Like it or not, that's how he rolled. But with Cassie, well, there was something more.

Plus, he'd seen those jerks glaring at her in the courtroom. Maybe they'd decided dirty looks weren't enough and they wanted to do something to her.

The ringing coming through the speaker stopped. Leon reached over to disconnect rather than listen to the call go to her voice mail again. But just before he tapped the screen, he heard the static sound of a bad connection, the sound of someone breathing, and then, very quietly, Cassie said, "I'm beside the stream just past the bridge." The connection wasn't good, and parts of her words kept cutting off as she continued talking. He made out something about her being shot at, heading east, the shooter being in the woods surrounding her, and what might have been a warning for him to be careful.

The call dropped and his fear-fueled pounding heart seemed to drop along with it. Was she hurt? Was the shooter tracking her? Did he dare call her back? Would the ringtone or the light from the phone screen give her location away to whoever was after her?

Leon's chest and stomach felt like one big knot as he barreled toward the bridge and Cassie. She could be in pain. She was probably terrified. And, knowing Cassie, she was probably angry, too. Leon wished he'd been able to tell her he was on his way. Give her at least that tiny bit of comfort and hope. But the fact that she'd warned him told him she knew he'd get to her side as soon as he could.

He punched 9-1-1 and gave the operator Cassie's general location, the situation she was in and a warning about a possible shooter at large. His headlights shining through the pouring rain swept across the bridge railings as he drove over it, and then he saw Cassie's SUV flipped on its roof, in the mud a good fifteen or twenty feet past the edge of the pavement. It had just barely stopped short of hitting a clump of pine trees. An impact with those could have been fatal.

Fear for Cassie made it hard for Leon to breathe. But then he quickly shoved his emotions aside. He disconnected the 9-1-1 call even though the operator had told him to stay on the line. He would need to be silent in the woods. If he was going to take any chances with using a phone, it would be in communication with Cassie. He had to find her and he knew he would have to take some risks to speed up the search.

In the meantime, he turned off his headlights, slowed and pulled off the road near Cassie's SUV. He cut the engine, grabbed his phone and pocketed it, and reached across the seat for his holster and gun. He leaned down and dug into his duffel bag on the floor for his night-vision binoculars, looped them around his neck and then grabbed a first-aid pouch that he could snap to his belt. He scanned the area with the binoculars but didn't see anybody. Then he shoved open the door, stepped out into the rain and took off jogging into the woods.

Just before he reached the stream, he dropped down behind a tree and grabbed the binoculars to take a quick look around. The last thing he wanted to do was to lead any lurking thug toward Cassie. He didn't see anybody. That, of course, did not mean there wasn't somebody out there.

His bounty hunting instincts prompted him to try to think like the person he was tracking. The water in the stream wasn't very deep and walking in it wouldn't leave tracks. That's the way Cassie would have gone. He stepped into the water and started slogging upstream, half expecting her to pop out from behind a tree on the stream bank.

He went several yards when he heard the crack of a rifle followed by the snap of a tree branch as it split from the trunk and tumbled downward, stopping before it completely broke free. The shooter must have seen him. Leon got out of the stream, sprinted into the woods and dropped down behind a tree to take out his binoculars again. He spotted the shooter, who was tilting his head slightly as he looked around. Leon couldn't see his face clearly due to the hat and covering he wore. But he could see a scope on the rifle as the shooter lifted his weapon to look through it. So the assailant had night vision, too.

Leon's phone vibrated. Keeping it hidden in his pocket so the glare wouldn't show, he moved it so he could see the screen. It was a text from Cassie.

Heard a shot. You okay?

He took his shot and missed, Leon replied.

Cassie texted back, Sounds like you're still downstream from me. I'll start heading in your direction.

No. He's got a night vision scope. Stay where you are. I'll come to you.

Leon trusted that if she had her own night-vision equipment, she'd let him know.

His phone vibrated again and he checked her reply.

OK.

He was fairly certain he was on the same side of the stream that she was. Now he just had to find her without bringing the shooter along with him. He surveyed his surroundings with the binoculars. The gunman was just across the stream, looking in the direction of the split tree branch. Looking for Leon, and ultimately for Cassie.

Leon had to make sure he got to her first. He flattened on his belly and began crawling in Cassie's direction, ignoring the soaked pine straw, weeds and rocks, and sometimes having to hold his breath to keep from inhaling mud or rainwater. He crawled for several yards, stopped and used the binoculars again. The gunman was paralleling him. He was well equipped and smart. He'd obviously figured out that Leon was there to help Cassie.

Leon had to get to her before that guy did. Or he needed to lure the shooter away from her so she could make her way back to the road and to the cops who should be showing up any minute now.

Making himself the target and drawing away the gunman actually made more sense. He would leave his night-vision binoculars on the stream bank for Cassie to use. She wouldn't be safe if she had to run through the forest virtually blind. He'd find some prominent land feature to describe where he'd left them. That should work.

The rain started pattering down again and there was a flash of lightning as he sent a text to Cassie sketching out the basics of his plan. He waited for a reply. Two or three minutes passed and it felt like an eternity. Fear started to set in. Maybe the text hadn't gone through. Maybe she'd been significantly injured in the car crash. Maybe worse. He checked the screen again.

And then from the darkness he heard the words, "Fat chance."

Cassie.

She crept up and dropped down behind the tree into the mud beside him.

Thank You, Lord, Leon prayed silently, feeling the heavy weight and tight clutch of fear lift from him. They weren't out of the woods yet. Literally. But she was alive and well enough to move on her own. Being near her and seeing her face made him feel better. Just like it always did.

"I see you didn't stay in place," Leon grumbled. What he wanted to do was to wrap her in his arms. But that was not the nature of their relationship. And, fortunately, Leon had several years' experience in holding back on his feelings and impulses around her.

She wiped her wet hair out of her eyes. "I had to come find you before you got yourself killed. You thought I'd let you draw the shooter to you while I saved my own hide? Like I said, fat chance."

He looked away, hiding the faint smile that crossed his lips despite the dire situation. He should have predicted she wouldn't like the plan. "Has the shooter said anything to you? Do you have any idea who it is?" he asked.

A bullet splintered the tree trunk above their heads before she could answer. Someone had shot at them from the forest on their side of the stream. That meant the shooter Leon had been keeping track of had crossed over and circled around behind them. Or the shot could mean there was more than one gunman.

Leon moved around the tree to look across the stream with his binoculars. Shots fired from that direction confirmed that the original shooter was over there, so that answered the question. "There are at least two shooters," he whispered. "One on each side of the stream."

"We obviously can't stay here," Cassie responded.

"No," Leon said. "And I don't like the idea of trying to hide deeper in the forest. We don't know how many shooters there are. They could surround us. We need to head back downstream, toward the road. The cops should be showing up at any minute. Or, if they aren't there, and we can make it to my truck, we can get in it and drive away."

"Walking in the streambed will take us to the road the fastest," Cassie said. "Of course, that also means we'll stick out like a couple of sore thumbs."

Leon risked a quick glance at his phone, intending to call 9-1-1 to see how far out the cops were. It didn't look like he had any bars. So, no connection. A sudden barrage of bullets had him shoving the phone away. He grabbed his gun and fired in the directions of the two known shooters, driving them to dive and take cover. And then he grabbed Cassie's hand. "We've got to go. Now!"

They struggled to run through the weeds and soft mud, and then finally splashed into the streambed. When they'd gone several yards downstream and Leon felt certain the gunmen were behind them, he tucked his gun into his waistband and half pulled, half carried Cassie until he had her in front of him so that he shielded her body with his. If they meant to shoot her, they'd have to go through him.

Running down the streambed, Leon could hear the crack of rifle shots behind him, followed by the zing of bullets ricocheting nearby.

Just before the stream curved around a bend, Leon pushed Cassie forward, whirled around and fired several shots, hoping to buy some time for her to run further ahead.

He turned back around and made it past the curve, where red and blue lights flashed through the trees. Help was nearby, but it hadn't reached them yet. Cassie kept running for the road and the cop cars, and Leon did, too.

He heard the crack of one more shot and felt a bullet tear through his jacket, narrowly missing his left hip. He kept running and saw that Cassie had reached the spot where the stream passed through a culvert. From there, it flowed under the pavement and then emptied into Lake Bell. She staggered partway up the weed-covered bank toward the half dozen cops moving around near their patrol cars.

Leon caught up to her and she held out her hand. He reached for it, and she pulled him up the bank for the final few steps until they made it to the road.

Thank You, Lord, he prayed as the officers approached and began questioning Cassie. Relief coursed through him, but at the same time he still felt unsettled. The attack on Cassie was not really over. He was sure of it.

She might be safe for the moment. But somebody really *really* wanted her dead.

TWO

"I suppose anybody I've ever put handcuffs on and hauled back to jail could potentially be a suspect," Cassie said to Sergeant Gabe Bergman as he sat in front of her. "You know how it is when your job involves locking up criminals. The list of people who want to take their anger out on you gets pretty long." She leaned back on the sofa, arms crossed over her chest, and willed the warmth from the nearby crackling fire to sink into her body. A hot shower and change into dry clothes had not yet managed to put an end to her trembling.

Of course, the shaking could have less to do with being cold and more to do with fear. She was safe right now in the living room of her family home, North Star Ranch, with several tough, competent people around her. But a little over an hour ago, at least two people had been hunting her in the forest, trying to *kill* her. She'd been shot at by a fleeing bail jumper before, and she'd been in plenty of physical altercations, but she'd never been through anything like this.

If Leon hadn't shown up when he had, the situation could have turned out much differently. She glanced over to where he stood near the fireplace, listening in on her conversation with the sergeant.

Her dad, Adam, was also in the room, sitting grim-faced beside her on the sofa. Rock Solid Bail Bonds had a storefront office in downtown Stone River not far from the police station and courthouse. But Cassie also had a home office with several desks, printers and computers in a large room at the back of the ranch house.

Harry and Martin, who'd showed up at the ranch shortly after Cassie and Leon arrived, had already headed to the back office to compile a list of active cases to give to the sergeant. Jay and Sherry Laughlin, the husband-and-wife team who helped Adam run the ranch, had gone into the kitchen to brew coffee and set aside the dinner that no one felt like eating right now.

Sergeant Bergman, a detective with the Stone River Police Department, kept his unreadable cop gaze locked on Cassie. "Right now, who's on your short list of people who want to kill you and would actually try to do it?"

"Bryan Rogan's friends who were in the courthouse today," Leon interjected. "They were giving Cassie the evil eye because they knew she was there to give testimony against Rogan that could finally get him locked up for a significant amount of time."

"Those guys are idiots," Cassie said.

"Idiots can be deadly." Bergman looked down to tap something into the tablet he'd brought with him. "I have an idea of who Rogan hangs out with, but who exactly did you see in the courthouse?"

Cassie gave him the names of the three men.

"We'll have patrol go by their homes. You and I both know the bars where they tend to hang out, so we'll check there, too. See if they've broken with their usual pattern of behavior tonight. See if there's any apparent evidence that they were out in the woods in the rainstorm an hour ago."

"Maybe you'll spot a couple of them with pinecones in their hair," Cassie muttered.

Bergman looked up from the tablet. She thought she saw a hint of amusement in his eyes, but maybe not. Cassie used humor to deal with stress. All of her team did. The sergeant was definitely one of the good guys, but it was a challenge to get him to crack a smile.

"You didn't get a glimpse of the perpetrators' vehicle?" Bergman asked. "We didn't find anything on the scene. Maybe somebody dropped them off. You sure nobody drove by you in the seconds after the shots were fired while you were fighting to keep your SUV from going off the bridge?"

Cassie shook her head. "Nobody drove by. The original shooter was on foot. I'm sure of it. Positioned just beyond the bridge. Waiting for me." That bit of dark humor she'd been using to try to boost her spirits had already vanished, and the cold realization of what could have happened had settled back in.

The sergeant shifted his attention to Leon. "Did you see a vehicle parked by the side of the road? Anybody pass you while you were arriving to help Cassie?"

Leon tilted his head slightly, considering the question. "I don't remember seeing anybody."

Bergman nodded. "Patrol had a couple of cars checking the road in both directions as part of their initial response. They didn't come across anything suspicious."

"So, no sightings of an accomplice in the vicinity," Leon said.

"And so far, no vehicle."

"There's a fire road that winds around through the forest up that way," Cassie's dad said as Sherry and Jay walked into the living room from the kitchen carrying trays with coffee-filled mugs.

"We'll check out the fire road by air at first light tomorrow morning, assuming the storm has passed by then," Bergman said, grabbing a mug of coffee and taking a sip of it after everyone else had gotten theirs. "Otherwise, if it's still stormy, we'll get some all-terrain vehicles up there to look around."

"The shooters could already be long gone," Adam said. "And any tire tread evidence is certain to have washed away with all this rain."

"True," Bergman replied. "But we're still going to get out there to take a look."

"It might not be such a bad thing if the shooters *are* long gone," Leon said quietly, his gaze settling on Cassie.

"Are you kidding?" Cassie said, genuine surprise making her words come out louder than she'd intended. "I want them captured and locked up. Right now."

"But they're *not* captured," Leon said evenly. "They knew when you'd be driving over the bridge. Somebody must have been watching you and called to tell their accomplices when you left the courthouse and headed home. Or else they put a tracker on your car. This attack wasn't done on impulse. These aren't people who are just going to go away after one failed attempt."

"You think they're going to try to kill me again. And that they'll do it soon," Cassie said.

Leon nodded. "The curve in the road and the stream where we last saw them isn't far from here. It's possible they're already headed in this direction. Or that they'll come to the ranch eventually."

"If we don't catch them first," Cassie said.

"If *we* don't catch them first," Bergman interjected. "Finding whoever committed this crime and bringing them to justice is the job of the *police*. You are bounty hunters." His gaze took in both Cassie and Leon. "You have every right to defend yourselves. And if it turns out that someone out on bail was part of this, they've obviously violated their bond with this criminal behavior and you can go after them. But chasing down the people who attacked you tonight on your own is not something I can allow."

"Of course," Cassie said. She knew the rules and she played by them. She was not a law enforcement officer. But she knew her town. She had good connections that included people who would help her but who would never ever, for various reasons, talk to the cops. She could collect information and pass it along to Bergman. She'd done it before.

Harry and Martin entered the room from the home office. "I just sent you an email with a list of all of our current open cases for bail jumpers," Harry said to Bergman. "And I added a few of our recently written larger bonds for some pretty dangerous or reckless criminals. They aren't in violation of their bonds at the moment, at least not that I know of, but I thought maybe the attack on Cassie was preemptive.

"Cassie's an excellent bounty hunter in her own right, with an excellent team, obviously." Harry glanced at the other bounty hunters in the room and smiled slightly before turning more serious. "Maybe somebody thought it would be a good idea to have some friends take her out of the picture *before* they jumped bail." He shrugged. "Just trying to think of every possibility."

"We were discussing the possibility of the shooters coming to the ranch," Leon said.

"Oh. So are we all staying here tonight then?" Martin, the youngest of the bounty hunters, asked. "I'll have Daisy come out here, too. The more, the merrier."

Cassie shook her head at Martin. "Go home. Have a nice dinner with your wife." She turned to Harry. "You, too. Spend the evening like you normally would with Ramona. And get some rest. Because I expect you both to be at work tomorrow morning just like normal."

"We're planning to keep a patrol car going back and forth on the road between town and the ranch tonight, anyway," Bergman said. "To keep an eye out for the shooters as well as to have a unit nearby in case there's trouble and you put in a 9-1-1 call."

"Thank you," Cassie said. That sounded reasonable. Rearranging everyone's lives when they didn't know for certain that the shooters were heading for the ranch seemed like too much. Exercising caution was helpful. Overreacting in fear was not.

Bergman got to his feet and glanced toward Cassie and Leon. "Is there anything either of you can think of to tell me that I didn't already ask you about?"

Both answered that there was not. They'd already given statements while sitting in Bergman's unmarked cop car at the crime scene. Then they'd addressed his follow-up questions here. Cassie felt like they'd covered everything.

"If some new detail comes to mind once your thoughts settle down, like maybe you realize you *do* remember seeing part of a vehicle or something about the shooters' appearance, let me know," the sergeant said just before he turned to leave.

Adam stood to walk Bergman to the door. "We keep all the security equipment here in good repair," he said to the sergeant. "But tonight I'll make sure someone is awake all night. Just to be certain."

"Not a bad idea," Bergman said before offering a general good-night to the room and walking out the door.

"You should go home, too," Cassie said to Leon.

He looked at her and shook his head. "I smell lasagna. I'm staying for some of that."

From the dining area, Sherry laughed. "Leon's right. I think it *is* time to dish up some food."

Adam invited Harry and Martin to stay for dinner, but each man was anxious to get home to his wife.

"How bad is the damage to your SUV?" Adam asked Cassie as he came back into the living room after seeing Harry and Martin out.

Her dad's favorite technique for dealing with stressful situations was to divert the topic to something more mundane. He'd done it when she was an adolescent fretting about mean kids at school. And also when she was a grown woman, in the months after her husband had died and she'd fallen into a tangle of dark emotions. She'd used it herself on many occasions when things were tense at the office or turned edgy while she and her team were on a stakeout.

"I had the cops radio Rusty to pick the SUV up," she said. "I'm sure I'll get a text from him sometime tomorrow with details on the repairs."

"Body work is expensive," Adam noted as he headed for the dining area to help set the table.

Cassie stood and went with him. Leon followed.

"You could stay home and work out of the office here tomorrow," Adam said once they were all seated at the table, ready to dig in.

Cassie breathed in the rich scents of lasagna and garlic bread and realized she was ravenous. "Dad, I've got to go into town. I don't know if the attack tonight had anything to do with Bryan Rogan's trial, but I am still determined to testify."

"I'll make sure she's not alone," Leon added.

They all joined hands. Cassie's dad was to her right. Leon to her left.

Adam spoke a blessing over the meal and, as everyone joined in at the final *Amen*, he squeezed her hand and seemed hesitant to let go. When Cassie lifted her bowed head to look at her dad, he still had hold of her hand and his eyes looked especially shiny.

"It's okay, Dad," she said, squeezing his hand and offering him a smile. "I'm safe." She'd been checked out by EMTs. The bullet that had struck her had creased her skin, but the injury, while painful, hadn't been deep enough to warrant stitches. The rollover had been jolting, but she hadn't felt that X-rays were necessary. "I'm sure I'll be a little sore tomorrow," she said, "but that's all. I'm fine."

He nodded and finally let go of her hand. But then he set his attention to the open laptop on a side table in the dining area. The split-screen images showed live feed from the security cameras at various locations on the property. At North Star Ranch, they were always security conscious.

"Sure you're fine," Adam said, turning to her and

nodding. But while his words sounded confident, his eyes were filled with worry.

"Have you been awake all night?" Cassie asked Leon as she walked into the home office well before sunup the next morning.

"Things have been quiet," he answered, deflecting her question. Yes, he had been there all night. He'd watched the security monitors on the laptop then gone outside to walk around the house and the nearby stables and barn every hour or so, just to make sure everything was as it should be and that all the motion-sensor lights were functioning properly.

Adam's dogs, a Great Dane mixed breed named Duke and a fluffy little creature that might be part Yorkie named Tinker, were lying by Leon's feet. Both opened their eyes and rose at the sound of Cassie's voice to sleepily walk to her. She obligingly bent to give them head scratches. The hounds looked ridiculous side by side because they were so different in size. Neither had a killer instinct, but each would bark if a stranger came around the house. Leon had kept an eye on their behavior throughout the night, considering them one more layer of protection.

After the dogs were petted and happy, Cassie tightened the belt on her bathrobe, walked over to the chair at her desk and sat. The dogs followed her. She and her dad each had a desk in the large room. The two other desks were for use by whomever needed one.

"Did you get any sleep?" Leon asked her.

Cassie was not known to be an early riser and it was now just after four in the morning. Her hair stuck up in different directions and she'd taken out her contact lenses and put on her black-rimmed glasses, which made her look like a cute nerd.

"You know how it is after somebody takes a shot at you. Or the day after you've been in a car wreck. As soon as you close your eyes, you start to see everything that happened play out in your mind again. Each time that mental replay started, I found myself trying to analyze what was flittering through my thoughts. I tried to look for any small detail my brain was dredging up." She tapped her hands on the desktop. "I'm not sure how much of the time I was asleep and dreaming or how much of the time I was actually awake, thinking and remembering."

"You want to have your say in court today," Leon said, "and I respect that. But afterward, maybe you could take a day or two off, catch up on your rest, and give the police time to catch a lead on whoever tried to kill us."

That would also give Leon time to check around to see what he could learn about who might have launched the attack. He understood there were lines not to be crossed and actions that only the police should take. And he would not overstep his bounds. But he would not just sit on the sidelines, either.

"I need coffee," Cassie grumbled. "Did you make any?"

"Yeah. But I already drank it all."

She stood. "I'll make a pot." She headed for the door and the dogs went with her. On her way out, she passed by a bookcase and stopped to pick up the framed photo of her late husband.

Leon watched her study the picture of the man she

had been married to for three years before his life had been tragically cut short by a still unknown killer.

Idaho State Trooper Jake Hollister had been everything Leon Bragg was not. A handsome man from a good family with a squeaky-clean background and a college education, Jake had played on his university's football team. He'd grown up south of Stone River, down in Boise. After becoming a state trooper, he'd been transferred to the regional office that serviced Stone River. He'd only been in town a couple of months when he'd met Cassie. They'd been married just before he'd become a detective.

Leon watched Cassie put the picture down and walk out. Soon after, he heard the sounds of cabinet doors being opened and water running as she made coffee.

From the desk where he was sitting, Leon gazed at the framed photo of Cassie's husband.

Leon came from a family of hard-drinking bar brawlers, thieves and drug addicts. He knew how to track down and deal with thugs because he'd been one. After bottoming out, he finally had a moment of mental clarity that had helped him realize his life didn't have to keep going in the same direction. Working his way to a cleaner, happier life had not been easy. He'd had his failures and relapses. But he had not given up.

Faith hadn't been mentioned in the household Leon had grown up in, nor among his adult friends. But he did have an uncle who was a Christian. And that uncle had been willing to extend Leon a helping hand when he'd needed it most. Leon, in turn, had found himself drawn to the faith that had made his uncle different from nearly everyone else he'd known.

Eventually, Leon had taken the life experience and

knowledge of criminal activity he'd once used for bad and turned it around to use for good. But even so, he was nothing like Jake Hollister. He realized that Cassie missed her husband and most likely wanted to find someone with whom she could rebuild her life. He hoped she would find the right man. And he'd accepted the fact that the right man would never be him.

The rich aroma of brewing coffee reached him as he scanned the security feeds on his computer screen and then glanced out the window. It was not quite sunrise yet. Lights on the ranch buildings illuminated the area around them for a short distance. Beyond that, everything was still dark. Thinking like a criminal, Leon realized that if he were going to launch an attack on the ranch house, *now* would be the time—when people inside the house were either still asleep or thought the threat of danger had passed. With that in mind, he figured it was probably a good time to take another look outside.

He got up and walked out into the hallway. He couldn't see the dogs in the kitchen, but he could hear their toenails tapping on the hardwood floor. Duke came around the corner to greet him first, tail wagging, a big crunchy bone-shaped treat in his mouth. Tinker skittered along behind him, his paws moving double-time to keep up with his doggie brother. He carried a much smaller treat in his mouth.

Cassie was moving toward the front door, coffee mug in hand, when Leon stepped in front of her to block her way. "I can take the dogs outside," he said. Given the potentially dangerous wildlife in the area, like bears and mountain lions, or the possibility of a smelly encounter with a skunk, the dogs weren't typically let out without someone keeping an eye on them.

"I'll do it," Cassie said. "I need some fresh air."

"Not a good idea." He realized that she wasn't unaware of the potential for danger. She simply didn't want to hide in the house and live in fear. But sometimes, for the short term, she would need to do exactly that.

"If somebody's waiting out there, they could just as easily take a shot at you as they could at me," Cassie said to him.

"Nobody's specifically targeting me. They only shot at me last night because I interrupted their plan and got in their way."

She sighed heavily. "Fine. You take the dogs out."

Leon's thoughts turned to her picking up the photo of her husband on her way out of the office. "Have you been doing some research into Jake's murder again?"

"You know I always am."

"Learn anything new? Maybe gotten a fresh lead you didn't tell Bergman about last night because you want to track it down yourself, first?"

She took a deep breath and blew it out. "In a way, I have. I didn't even think about it until I was tossing and turning in the middle of the night." She shook her head. "It's not related to the attack last night. I don't see how it could be. It's not even specific information. It's more like a rumor, which could ultimately turn out to be nothing, like so many of the other 'tips' I've gotten." She set her empty coffee mug on the end of the kitchen counter and then shoved her hands into the pockets of her bathrobe. "It could just be Phil Warner hustling me and trying to make a few extra dollars."

Phil was a paid informant who was sometimes helpful and sometimes unreliable. Any information from him had to be taken with a grain of salt.

"Phil got picked up for being drunk and disorderly. He told me he was tossed into the drunk tank with someone who'd been arrested for driving under the influence. That guy told Phil he hadn't been through Stone River in a long time. 'Not since the cop was killed.' And that, after that happened, he'd had to get out of town."

"Why'd he have to get out of town?"

Cassie shook her head. "I don't know. That's all Phil had to tell me. Maybe it's true. Maybe Phil just made the whole thing up because he wanted me to give him some money."

"How long ago did this happen?" Leon asked, forcing himself not to jump to conclusions even as his heart sped up. Maybe the person who murdered Cassie's husband would *finally* be brought to justice.

"Phil told me his story…" She glanced toward the living room window where there was a hint of daylight on the horizon. "Well, four days ago now. I haven't gotten anywhere with it. Phil didn't know the guy's name, so I looked up the public records on arrests for the date he gave me. There were three men picked up for driving under the influence that night. I did a quick search and none of the names sounded familiar to me. I've asked around a little bit—some people at the city jail and at the courthouse—but none of the three names meant anything to anybody. My next step will be to get the mug shots of all three men and show them to Phil, to see if he can identify the guy."

"Maybe your asking around about those men triggered the attack."

Cassie shrugged. "Anything's possible, I guess, but that wouldn't make much sense. It takes a lot to build a murder case. Certainly more than the ramblings of a drunk in a jail cell. There's still virtually no physical evidence for the case. So I don't see how my asking questions could lead to the over-the-top assault we went through. Somebody's already kept a cool head and gotten away with murder for five years. Why take a huge risk like the attack last night?"

She took her hands out of her bathrobe pockets. "But I will mention it to Sergeant Bergman. Maybe he can help me get some information on the mystery man later, after things calm down. For now, though, my priority will be to focus on the cases we're currently working, the people who have threatened me in the past, and most especially the thugs who are angry about me testifying at Bryan Rogan's trial." With that, she picked up her empty coffee mug and headed back into the kitchen toward the coffeepot.

Leon walked outside, chilled by the air and by his worry for Cassie while the dogs barked and bounded around him. Last night's attack could have been motivated by many things. He didn't want to let himself get caught in the trap of deciding what he thought had happened and then look for evidence to prove it. He wanted to keep an open mind.

Still, the murder of an Idaho law enforcement officer was a big deal. Jake's case had sadly run cold due to a lack of leads, not to a lack of interest. But now, because of the questions Cassie had recently been asking, maybe somebody thought she knew something. Something big. And maybe that somebody thought she needed to be silenced.

THREE

"What's the name of your informant?" Sergeant Bergman asked.

Cassie looked at the desk phone in the Rock Solid Bail Bonds downtown Stone River office, where the detective's voice came through the speaker. She'd just told him the details about the possible lead to her husband's killer after explaining that she thought the odds of it being related to the attack on her last night were relatively small.

She hesitated to answer and glanced at Leon, who was seated at his nearby desk, watching her. It was just the two of them in the office right now. Harry and Martin had already left to set up surveillance on a house where they thought a bail jumper might be hiding.

Cassie had a standing agreement with Phil that she would not tell anyone he sold her information. But based on what she'd already relayed, the detective was bound to figure out who her informant was anyway. Why draw things out and make it more difficult for him?

"His name is Phil Warner," she said.

"All right. I'll check around on this when I can. Right now, my priority is finding our suspects for last night's attack."

"Of course," Cassie said flatly, trying not to feel deflated. When Phil had first given her the information, she'd tried not to get her hopes up that Jake's killer would finally be found. It was a self-protective mechanism she'd developed over the years after being disappointed so many times before. And yet, maybe this person who'd been locked up with Phil really could lead them to something that would ultimately result in the capture of his killer.

She heard Bergman sigh through the speaker. "We haven't forgotten about Jake," he said in a firm, steady voice. "He was one of our own and we haven't been just passively waiting for information about his murder to come our way. But sometimes it takes time for the truth to come out."

And sometimes the truth never comes out. Cassie heard the words in her head even though he hadn't said them aloud. She'd worked around law enforcement long enough to know it was true. Justice did not always prevail.

She nodded, even though they were on the phone and he couldn't possibly see her. But she didn't trust herself to speak. Her heart was in her throat as she pictured Jake in her mind's eye. The hard knot of painful emotion had snuck up on her. Jake was gone and he wasn't coming back. She knew that. And finding his killer would not bring him back. It would not change the facts of the situation at all, really. Whatever happened with the investigation into his death, she needed to move on with her life. But she couldn't.

She took a couple of deep breaths while looking down at her desktop, pulling herself together so she could continue to sound like a professional while talking with the detective.

The sound of boot steps on the office's hardwood floor made her look up, and she found herself gazing into Leon's dark brown eyes. His compassionate expression was still not enough to soften a tough-looking face that had weathered some pretty rough times. He set a steaming mug of coffee in front of her and, of all things, a laugh came out of her mouth. Because this one little mundane gesture was *exactly* what she needed to get that emotional lump out of her throat. Aside from that, she'd had a pounding headache for the last hour. Coffee would probably help ease that.

"I know the Stone River Police Department is doing all it can to find Jake's killer," she said into the phone before taking a sip of coffee. "And I appreciate it." *And I know with more and more people moving into the area and the police department staying roughly the same size, you're overextended trying to take care of current crime.* Again, she had her ideas on the truth of the situation, but she didn't say them. Because it would come out sounding like a criticism, which wasn't her intention.

"Getting back to the attack on you last night, I'm not assuming it is or is not connected to what you just told me," Bergman said. "Right now, I'm focused on collecting all the facts."

"Of course."

"The rain that's been hanging around for the last couple of days is finally slacking off, but the cloud cover is still too low for the sheriff's department to send out their helicopter," he continued. "If the clouds don't lift pretty soon, we'll dispatch somebody on an ATV to take a look at the fire roads through that area. Since we didn't spot a suspect vehicle when our officers first arrived on scene, or locate one after you were rescued and the perpetrators vanished, I'm curious to see if there's any sign that the fire road was the route our bad guys used to arrive and depart."

"Do you really think you could find any evidence after last night's storm?" Cassie asked.

"It's a long shot, but long shots pay off sometimes. That land is a hodge-podge of private and government-owned property. There's a forest service facility not too far from there and some small cabins. Somebody might have seen or heard something last night. Locals might have noticed people tromping around, scouting the location days before the attack. It would be difficult to do something like that without leaving a shred of evidence."

But someone killed my husband without leaving any evidence. Cassie took a deep breath, reminding herself that the deep wave of cold sorrow she felt at the moment was probably a case of the new trauma of the attack dredging up the old trauma of her husband's homicide. All of these feelings about Jake's murder that were bubbling up should settle back down eventually. Unless her lead on the jailhouse confession did turn into something. If the investigation became active again, most likely her emotions would be all over the place.

"Even though Bryan Rogan's friends who were glaring at you in the courthouse turned out to have solid alibis for the time you were attacked last night, I've requested the bailiffs keep a close eye on them and to keep their behavior in line while they're in the courthouse."

Earlier this morning, Bergman had sent Cassie a text to let her know that the men who'd been trying to intimidate her in court the day before had airtight alibis for the time of the attack. They'd gone out to eat. Not only did they have eyewitnesses to confirm their story, there was video camera time-stamped footage proof, as well.

"You are still planning to testify today, right?" Bergman asked.

"Of course. The prosecutor checked in with me to make sure I was okay. After I told her that I was, she asked me to be at the courthouse by ten. I'd better get going."

"Well, watch yourself on your way over there and back. Just because the goons from the viewing gallery have alibis doesn't mean the attack didn't come from Bryan Rogan's criminal friends. Maybe the gallery guys were a diversionary setup of some kind to get us looking in the wrong direction. Things aren't always what they appear to be at first glance."

"I know that only too well," Cassie said.

After Bergman disconnected, Cassie finished the last of her coffee and then stood, biting back a groan as several muscles and tendons in her back made their presence known. The SUV rollover last night had jarred her body and this morning she was really feeling it. She pulled open her bottom desk drawer and took out her satchel-style purse. Then she opened the office safe so she and Leon could store their handguns inside. They wouldn't be allowed to bring them into the courthouse. And Cassie had a strict policy against leaving guns unattended in a vehicle where anyone—including a dangerous criminal—could break a window or pop open a trunk or rear hatch to get at them.

"Given what happened last night, I'm not real thrilled at the thought of going anywhere unarmed," Leon said.

"We're heading in the direction of the government buildings and police station. Somebody would have to be pretty desperate to take a crack at me over there."

Leon looked at her, his face solemn. "They seem pretty desperate to me."

He had a point.

They locked up the office and went out the back to the small parking lot. Cassie took in a deep breath of cool, clean air and looked around at the nearby redbrick buildings and the mountains with their cloud-shrouded peaks. Most of the time, Cassie liked to walk the short distance to the courthouse. But the creepy sensation of having a target painted on her back meant that today she was happy to ride in Leon's truck instead.

While making the short drive, Cassie placed a quick call to Harry to see how he and Martin were doing with their surveillance. She brushed aside Harry's concern for her and directed the conversation back to the topic at hand, at the same time scanning the area around them as Leon drove. Harry sounded fairly confident that they'd found the location where their target, a bail jumper who'd been busted for drug possession with intent to sell along with assault and resisting arrest charges, had been hiding out over the last couple of days. But he wasn't completely certain if the guy was there right this minute.

"Since it's only the two of you and the fugitive's known to be violent, I don't want you trying to take him down until Leon and I can get there." Martin's wife, Daisy, was a bounty hunter who'd recently come to work for Rock Solid Bail Bonds after marrying Martin. But she'd taken off the day to visit her mom and aunt over in Montana. It was her aunt's birthday and

Daisy had asked for the day off a week ago. "Stay out of sight," Cassie said to Harry. "I'll call you as soon as Leon and I get out of court."

She disconnected just as Leon parked and cut the engine. They took their time scanning the area for anyone suspicious-looking before getting out of the vehicle and heading toward the white-columned building. As they walked up to the metal detector inside, they powered down their phones.

"You got a few looks at the original shooter through your night-vision binoculars last night," she said to Leon after they passed through screening and headed for the courtroom. "If he's here today, sitting with Rogan's loser friends, do you think you might recognize him? Possibly by his eyes or posture or the way he moves?"

"I'll give it a try."

Right now, anything was worth a try. Cassie was certain another attack was imminent. But she didn't know which direction it would come from. Were the attackers friends of Bryan Rogan's or were they somehow connected to Jake's murder? Maybe they were people with a motivation she knew nothing about.

If Leon had his way, Cassie would go back to the ranch and stay there until the shooters from last night were captured. But he knew she was not likely to do that. Instead, she refused to be intimidated and continued to do everything she could to take crime off the streets. Her attitude scared him, since it put her in danger, but he admired her courage. And if he were in her shoes, he wouldn't want to hide, either.

He glanced over her as they left the courtroom. They'd been inside for a couple of hours, and during that time Leon had taken several good looks at Bryan Rogan's friends, who were once again in the gallery watching the proceedings. When the judge had declared a short recess and they'd stood from their seats, there was nothing familiar about their stature or the way they moved. Nothing to make him think there was a connection to last night's attack.

Shortly after court resumed, Cassie had been called to testify. She'd talked about Rogan's violent behavior while she and her bounty hunters had been tracking him. She'd recounted his attack on Martin and how Martin had wrestled the knife away just before Rogan could plunge it into his chest. Only, Rogan had grabbed a second knife hidden in his boot and sliced it across Harry's forearm as he'd attempted to help bring Rogan under control. She'd also relayed the specific death threats Rogan had made against Cassie, her dad and her bounty hunters.

When she'd finished testifying and the judge had dismissed her, she and Leon walked out into a blustery, mostly sunny day with just a few dark clouds on the horizon.

"I'm starving," Leon said. "Let's stop by the Bear Hollow Deli and pick up some sandwiches. Harry and Martin got an early start. They're probably hungry, too."

"Text them to see what they want," Cassie responded. "I'm buying."

"I'm not going to tell them you're buying," Leon said. "They'll order one of everything on the menu."

Cassie laughed in response.

Both kept their heads moving and their glances sweeping across the area as they walked to the truck, mindful of potential danger. Once they were inside, they checked their phones.

"Looks like I've got a voice mail from Sergeant Bergman and one from Harry," Cassie said.

She connected to the truck's hands-free system and played Bergman's first message. "Hi, Cassie. We found a car bogged down in the mud on the fire road near where you were attacked. The registered owner is Jerry Lutz. I know he was one of the original suspects in Jake's murder. Lutz reported the car stolen about seven days before you were attacked. I'm going now to talk to him."

Leon looked at Cassie, his heart beating a little more rapidly in his chest at the possibility that the shooters from last night might quickly be found *and* that there might finally be a break on the murder of Jake Hollister. He could see the color draining from Cassie's face. His impulse was to reach out and take her hand, but he didn't dare. That was a line the two of them did not cross. Instead, he cleared his throat and glanced around the parking lot, giving her a moment to collect her emotions.

"So, if I remember correctly, this Jerry Lutz guy that Bergman mentioned was a suspect early on because he had a beef against Jake."

"That's right," Cassie said, her voice sounding a little scratchy as if she might be holding back tears. "Lutz was stealing cars, dismantling them and selling the parts online. He had quite the business going, with four other people working for him. Jake worked undercover on that case and helped bust him.

"Lutz didn't have any priors, so he got a fairly short sentence, but by the time he was released from prison, his wife had left him. He decided Jake had ruined his life and he threatened to get his revenge on him. Not too long after that, Jake was murdered. But there was no physical evidence that proved Lutz had killed him." She cleared her throat. "Maybe we'll find that evidence now. Or at least have a witness."

"So you think Lutz heard about you asking questions based on what Phil told you, and he got a buddy to help him kill you before he got caught and sent to prison for the murder?"

Cassie shrugged and looked away. But not before Leon could see the teardrops fall from her lower eyelashes. She hurriedly wiped them away and he felt his heart break a little. He could only imagine what she was feeling right now.

"Are you going to call Bergman back?" he asked, knowing that some overt gesture of sympathy or soft words would *not* make Cassie feel better. She'd made it clear many times that she didn't care for platitudes. Leon had learned that just being with her seemed to be what helped her the most. That, and sometimes moving things along without dwelling on the moment when she was obviously feeling emotionally vulnerable. "Bergman left that message nearly an hour ago. He may have more information by now."

Cassie shook her head. "He called me while he was in the middle of an active investigation with a hot lead to follow up on. That was a big favor. I don't want to repay him by calling him back and asking him for something more while he's busy." She took a deep breath and let it out. Then she finally turned and looked directly Leon, letting him see the stormy emotions in her eyes. "He'll call again when he has answers."

Leon took a deep breath, wishing he could do something to make her feel better.

Cassie played the voice mail message from Harry. "Our bail jumper wasn't in the house before, but he is now. He just drove up and went inside. I don't know how long he'll stay in place, so we need to make the bust as soon as you can get here. Call me when you get out of court."

"We'll have to go to the deli later," Cassie said to Leon. "I don't want to risk losing this guy."

"Understood." He backed the truck out of the slot and headed for the parking lot exit.

"I'll let them know we're on our way." Cassie tapped out a text message and sent it. Then, after checking her phone for the information she needed, she put the exact address they were headed for into the truck's GPS system.

Fifteen minutes later, they were turning onto the street near the house where Harry and Martin had located the bail jumper. Leon spotted Harry's truck and drove up to park behind it. Harry and Martin got out, already wearing bulletproof vests and clearly ready to go.

As Leon and Cassie exited his truck, he couldn't help noticing that Cassie was moving more slowly and stiffly than usual. Maybe he hadn't noticed earlier because he'd been so focused on keeping an eye on their surroundings. Clearly, the car wreck and assault had taken a lot out of her physically.

"You always tell us not to work if we're hurt," he said quietly as they walked to the back of his truck where he lifted the latch on the compartment so they could grab their bulletproof vests. Since their guns were back in the office, they would have to count on Harry and Martin for firepower if it was needed. "Maybe you should stay back this time," he added. "Let the rest of us handle this one."

Harry and Martin approached before she responded.

"The good news is, there's fencing on both sides of the property," Martin said after a quick greeting. "And the backyard extends to an inlet with no dock or boat or anything this guy could use to escape."

"So, not too many directions he can run off to without having to slow down to get past some kind of barrier," Cassie said.

Harry nodded. "It should be pretty easy to corral him if he tries to run. And I'm fairly certain he's alone in there."

"I'll stand at the end of the driveway so I can see what happens if he does make it all the way to the street," Cassie said.

"Sounds good," Harry said.

Leon gave both Harry and Martin a slight nod of approval. It wasn't like Cassie to place herself away from the action. They'd obviously noticed that she wasn't moving around as easily as usual, but weren't making a big deal about it.

Everybody took a minute to do a quick radio check and take one more look at the fugitive's mug shot.

"Okay," Leon said, "Harry and I will take the front door. Martin, you run around back. Cassie, watch the street. Let's get this guy."

The three men pushed their way through the thick pine trees that covered the property in front of the house, making a beeline for the porch. Martin split off and ran alongside of the house toward the back.

Leon bounded up the steps to the front door. Harry

stood behind him and a little to the side where he'd have a wider view of anything happening around the front of the house.

Leon knocked on the door. A fair percentage of the time, if he knocked normally rather pounding, people actually opened the door. While waiting for a response, he felt the rush of adrenaline that tensed his muscles and sharpened his senses. He couldn't hear anything from inside the house. Not even the sound of a TV or music playing. He gave it a second and knocked again.

A couple of minutes passed with no response and he began to wonder if anyone was really in there. He glanced at Harry, who pointed at the door and nodded vigorously, as if he knew what Leon was thinking and wanted to confirm that he knew for certain the fugitive was inside.

Leon finally pounded on the door, ready to escalate the situation and do whatever it took to apprehend this dangerous fugitive.

Finally, he heard someone moving around inside the house. And then the door opened and the guy was standing there, bleary-eyed and rubbing his face.

"Louis Hader, you missed your court date," Leon said. "You've violated bail and we're here to take you in."

Hader stared at him for a moment, still either half asleep or high. Leon couldn't tell for certain. "I couldn't get a ride to the courthouse," the bail jumper finally said.

"The reason why you didn't show up doesn't matter. We've got to take you in and get this taken care of."

Hader started to retreat into the house, a sly expression on his face. "I'll go later today, before the court closes."

Leon stepped onto the threshold so Hader couldn't slam the door in his face and shook his head. "Later won't work. We've got to go now."

Hader's eyes widened in panic. He looked beyond Leon, like he might actually be considering trying to run past him and flee. But then he apparently saw Harry waiting nearby and realized making an escape wouldn't be so easy. Finally, he rubbed his shaved head and sighed. "I need to put on my shoes first."

Leon motioned Harry forward and they followed Hader inside the house, where they quickly made certain no one else was lurking. They waited for him to put on his shoes before cuffing him. After a quick check to make certain the doors and windows were locked and the building secured, they headed out the front door. Leon kept control of their captive fugitive while Harry radioed Martin and Cassie to let them know their bail jumper had been captured and the situation was secure.

Martin responded and came around from the back to join them at the front of the house. The bounty hunters and their fugitive headed down the driveway toward the street to meet up with Cassie. But when they got there, she was nowhere in sight.

Immediately feeling sick with worry, Leon grabbed his radio and asked her for her location. There was no response. He did it three more times. But his radio remained silent.

FOUR

"What do you want with me?" Cassie demanded of the masked man pointing a gun at her.

"Shut up!" he snapped, shoving her toward the open door of the van parked on the street around the corner from bail jumper Louis Hader's house.

Climbing into that van was the absolute last thing Cassie wanted to do, but what choice did she have? She'd been standing at the edge of Hader's property when two assailants had moved silently through the trees and gotten the drop on her. One of them had been clever enough to point his gun at Leon and Harry as they'd made contact with Hader, threatening to kill Cassie's bounty hunters if she didn't keep her mouth shut and come with them. She wasn't about to let Leon or Harry be shot for the sake of her own safety, so she'd cooperated with the masked men's demands.

They were likely the two who'd tried to kill her last night. It was odd that they hadn't killed her as soon as they'd seen her today. The only reason she could figure for that was that they didn't want the group of bounty hunters in the vicinity chasing them as soon as they heard the shot. So the kidnappers probably intended to take her into the nearby forest, shoot her and dump her body there.

So far they'd hustled her down the street and around the corner, using the cover of the trees with efficient precision. Maybe these guys were professionals. Her thoughts raced to the fugitives her team had recovered or helped to recover who were connected to organized crime, but there weren't many. Bail bond companies out of Los Angeles and Miami had asked for local help to recover fugitives who'd thought it would be easy to hide in a small town. Daisy and Martin, with a little help from Leon and Harry, had captured the Miami fugitives over in Montana. Cassie and Leon had quickly tracked down the fugitives who were hiding in Idaho. In the case that Cassie and Leon worked, there had been nothing especially dramatic about the capture. No reason for a grudge. And she'd just testified at Rogan's trial, so her theory that the attacks were intended to prevent her from giving her testimony didn't hold water anymore.

This *had* to be about Jake's murder. The attacks had started after she'd gotten that lead on a possible witness. At this point it seemed too much to believe that the timing of these attacks was simply coincidental.

She balked at the door of the van. "Wait, where are you taking me?"

They hadn't said much to her or to each other in front of her, and now she wanted to get them talking. She might recognize their voices. Or maybe something about the way they talked would give her a hint about who they were or where they were from. Maybe there actually was some kind of organized crime connection. But it had been Jake, not her, who'd made an enemy and that person had subsequently killed him. Maybe that enemy had gotten wind of Cassie's possible lead on her husband's killer and was worried about being found out.

"Move!" The thug shoved his gun into her side.

If she got into that van, she'd never get out alive. *Lord, give me strength and guidance.* If only she hadn't left her weapon in the safe back at the bail bonds office.

"If you take a shot at me, my bounty hunters will be on you in a heartbeat," she declared boldly, even as icy fear tightened its grip and she felt herself beginning to tremble. "They'll hear the shot and they'll come running." She could see their weapons weren't fitted with sound suppressors. "I'm sure they're already looking for me."

The creeps had taken her radio and tossed it aside when they'd grabbed her. Her phone was still in her pocket, but moving her hand toward it was too much of a risk while they were watching her so closely. She'd turned off the sound notifications just before the move to bust Louis Hader, something she typically did so a badly timed incoming call would not give away her location when she was trying to sneak up on a fugitive. It was in vibrate mode and she'd felt it going off several times now. Someone was trying hard to get hold of her. Probably Leon.

"People living on this street will hear the gunshot if you shoot me," she continued.

The gunmen must have been following her since the attack last night. Or maybe since she and Leon left the ranch this morning. She had the impression that this abduction might have been planned on the fly. Their goal of getting her away from the others and back to the van had worked well. But they hadn't looked at the bigger picture. Like the potential for witnesses in this residential neighborhood.

"If people hear gunshots on their street, they're going to look out the window," she continued, desperate to convince them to not just shoot her on the spot while she resisted getting into the van. "The local residents might not be able to see your faces because of the masks, but they'll see this van. And when they call the cops, the investigators will be able to track it down. They'll find images of it on security video. Lots of people have a home security camera outside their house. You're not going to get away with this."

The closest gunman glanced at his partner.

That's when Cassie tried to twist her upper body out of his grip while kicking at him.

Both thugs immediately grabbed her arms. Their grips were painfully tight.

She lifted her feet off the ground, hoping that the sudden weight of her body would throw them off balance, make them stumble, give her a chance to escape. But it didn't work. Despite her body dropping closer to the ground, they didn't lose their hold.

One of the abductors kept a hand on her arm while he tucked away his gun and then wrapped his free hand around her neck. The other shoved his gun into his waistband and reached for Cassie's feet.

She kicked and thrashed as hard as she could. She screamed, louder than she'd ever screamed in her life. Instantly, she felt a viselike pressure on her throat followed by a sudden sharp pain to the side of her head. And then everything went dark.

"Call the police and let them know Cassie might be in danger." Leon barked out the words as he ran to his truck.

"What about Louis?" Martin asked.

Leon quickly considered the question. His first thought was to let the bail jumper go. If they'd captured him once, they could capture him again. And Cassie was by far Leon's highest priority. But the possibility existed that Cassie was *not* in danger. That she was talking to someone and had chosen to ignore his radio calls and attempt to contact her by phone. That would be highly unusual behavior for her, but it was possible.

"Cuff him to the porch rail," he said. "Let the cops know where he is when you tell them about Cassie. They can send a patrol unit to come get him."

Harry, who'd been scouring the immediate area looking for Cassie, jogged up to Leon. "What's the plan?"

"We're going to find her and make sure she's okay," Leon said. "I had to secure my weapon in the safe at the office before going to court with Cassie. Give me your gun."

Harry pulled his handgun from his holster and handed it over.

Martin quickly cuffed the bail jumper and then hurried over to Leon and Harry, all while talking to a 9-1-1 dispatcher.

Harry gestured at the phone in Leon's hand. "Can you see Cassie on your phone's tracker app?"

Everyone on the Rock Solid Bail Bonds team was registered with the company's tracking app account. It was a basic security requirement. The problem was that, in a town like Stone River in the mountainous region between Idaho and Montana, reception could be iffy. And right now, as Leon looked at his phone, all he could see was a screen showing a partial map with several blank sections of missing data and an endlessly spinning wheel hovering over the top of it all.

"First thing we'll do is a quick look up and down the surrounding streets," Leon said. "You and Martin head south. I'll head north. As soon as one of us gets some useful data, we'll let each other know."

And, hopefully, when one of them did finally get a strong enough signal to see a location, it would show them where Cassie actually was in real time. Not just some spot where her phone had been tossed.

Leon yanked open his truck door, got inside and fired up the engine. His heart was pounding in his chest. Abductions and disappearances were terrifying. He'd worked a few of them, volunteering his services, along with other Rock Solid bounty hunters, to search local wilderness areas for a missing person.

It was one thing to directly square off against someone in a fight. You knew what you were up against and what you needed to do to take care of the dangerous situation. It was something else altogether when you didn't know which way to look. Didn't even know what had happened. And now he was facing that situation with Cassie. Her sudden disappearance when he knew someone was trying to kill her was the stuff of nightmares.

Lord, please protect her.

The wheel on the locater app on his phone was still spinning, so he connected to the hands-free device, tossed the phone onto the console alongside his radio, looked up at the road ahead of him and hit the gas.

The last time anyone had had contact with Cassie was roughly twenty minutes ago. If someone had grabbed her at about that time, they could be pretty far gone by now. They could have taken her deep into the wilderness.

Chill, he commanded himself. He had to stay cool if he wanted to find her. The police would be on the hunt for her, too. At the moment, he would stay close to her last known location and look for any clue that could tell him what had happened to her.

After he'd tried to call her several times and hadn't gotten a response, he couldn't make himself believe she was just ignoring his calls anymore.

He reached the end of the road and made a right turn. There, on the right a short distance from the corner, he saw a section of tall wild grass that had been recently tromped. Last night's rains had left the exposed dirt near the grass a mud pit and, in the mud, there were footprints and a tire tread.

He got out of his truck for a closer look, noting two sets of large footprints probably belonging to men. There was also a set of smaller prints, possibly belonging to a woman. Two men, like in the attack in the woods last night. And Cassie.

He reached for his phone as he climbed back into his truck. He wanted Harry to turn around and head in this direction while having Martin relay what Leon had seen to the police. But as he glanced at the screen he saw that the spinning wheel on the tracking app was gone. Instead, there was the familiar map of Stone River and a small dot identified as Cassie. And that dot was moving.

"Her tracker app shows her moving west on Cataldo Street," Leon said into his phone after connecting with Harry. That was the street Leon was already on. He punched the truck's gas pedal and started moving. The road was curvy and tree-lined so he couldn't see very far ahead. "I don't have a visual yet. Looks like she's about seven miles ahead of me."

Please let this be Cassie. Maybe it was her up ahead of him. But maybe whoever she was with had tossed her phone into the bed of a truck going in a completely different direction just to throw off anybody trying to find her.

"I'm on Ponderosa Street," Harry said. "I should reach the intersection with Cataldo just about the time you get there."

Through the speaker, Leon could hear the sound of Harry gunning his engine. And the sound of Martin relaying the information to the police via his phone. Good. Maybe the cops would be able to quickly set up a perimeter so the driver wouldn't get away.

Leon was frustrated that the curves in the road slowed him down, but at least they also slowed the vehicle he was pursuing. He tried to figure out where it was headed, but that was hard to say. They'd started in a part of town with residences somewhat widely spaced; now they were headed toward the more heavily populated area near downtown Stone River and the public beaches along Lake Bell.

Leon's truck had a powerful engine and big, deeply treaded tires that gave him high clearance. If they went off-road he could keep up with them. If they stayed on-road he'd definitely catch up with them. But he hadn't yet seen the vehicle he was pursuing. If they'd found Cassie's phone and tossed it, and then were able to get away without Leon seeing them, he wouldn't be able to tell the cops anything about the vehicle they were searching for.

He fought to shake off the dark thoughts creeping

up on him. Bounty hunting was all about paying attention to what was happening in front of you and anticipating what could happen next. You considered all the possibilities you could think of, made your best choice and then lived with the results.

Choices and results. He'd made some bad choices in his life, and some days it was hard to live with the results. Dark thoughts and connected emotions not even related to the pursuit at hand started slipping into his mind, all of them fueled by fear.

Again, he pushed himself to shake them off, to focus on something positive and helpful instead.

Cassie was smart, he reminded himself. She was strong. She was tough, even though she was kind of small. Leon would focus on those facts and drive the darkness out of his thoughts with the light of faith.

He needed to come up with a plan. If the police caught up with him by the time he found the bad guys, he'd let them take over and do their thing.

If not, Leon would take care of the situation. He couldn't just wait for someone else to arrive and complete the rescue mission. Not when Cassie's life was at stake.

He reached the intersection with Ponderosa Street and, as promised, Harry and Martin were there. Harry pulled onto the street behind Leon as soon as he passed by.

"Did you see a vehicle ahead of me as you drove up on the intersection?" Leon asked over the phone line he'd kept open after he'd called Harry a few minutes ago.

"No. Didn't see anybody."

There wasn't much traffic out here, but there would

be closer to town. According to the tracker app, Leon was closing in on Cassie's phone. And, hopefully, Cassie. He rounded a hairpin turn and there in front of him was an older yellow-and-tan camper van with a sleeping berth above the driver's area. A strategically placed thick swipe of mud covered the license plate.

The tracker showed Cassie's phone straight ahead. And since he wasn't looking at the bed of a truck where her phone could have been tossed to steer him chasing in the wrong direction, Leon was certain she was in there.

"This van is it," he said to Harry. "Cassie's in there."

Leon could hear Martin giving a description of the van and its location to the police.

The van had been going roughly the speed limit when Leon had first spotted it. Now, as he pulled up close behind, it began to speed up. Maybe the driver recognized Leon's truck. If the attackers had been stalking Cassie this morning, they would have seen it before and probably knew that it belonged to a bounty hunter.

"What do you want to do?" Harry asked.

Leon's first thought was to get in front of the van so that he and Harry could box it in and force it to stop.

"Cops should be here any minute," Martin reported.

The van took a sudden right turn, heading into a more densely populated neighborhood. Leon stayed on it, with Harry close behind. A sign announced a drop in the speed limit, but the van driver sped up even more.

"Get ready to box him in," Leon said to Harry. He couldn't hold off and wait for the cops to arrive and risk the van getting away.

Bang! Bang!

Somebody leaned out of the van's passenger-side

window and fired in Leon's direction as they passed a sign announcing that they were nearing a school with an adjacent park. There was no way Leon could return fire. Not only would he potentially put children in danger, but any bullet he fired could go through a window and strike Cassie.

"You okay?" Harry's voice came through the speaker.

"Yeah." Leon's focus stayed locked on the van. He would not let it get away. But he also didn't want to put Harry and Martin in further danger. "Slow down," he said to Harry. "Back off the pursuit."

"You back off, too," Harry snapped. "Getting yourself shot isn't going to help Cassie."

Leon wasn't going to back off.

Through his open window, he heard police sirens. Maybe the abductors heard the same thing. As the road hooked right, and the driver was forced to slow to make the curve, the side door on the van slid open and Cassie's body was tossed out, landing in the park and rolling down the hill.

Leon's heart nearly lurched out of his chest. Much as he wanted to catch the van and the dirtbags inside it, he wanted to take care of Cassie more. He pulled hard to the right, drove over the curb, across the sidewalk and ploughed down the grassy slope until he reached the spot where Cassie's body had come to rest. He leaped out of the truck and ran to her.

I'm too late. She's gone. Every horrible possibility ran through his head because terrible things did happen in life. He knew that for a fact.

She'd come to rest on her left side, reddish-blond hair fanned across her face, her arms and legs tucked in. Caught underneath her hands was a twisted plastic shopping bag. And then he saw that her ankles had been tied together with improvised binding made the same way, with twisted plastic shopping bags.

He was vaguely aware of Harry pulling up in his truck behind him, of hearing doors opening, and of hearing Martin request an immediate emergency medical response.

Leon dropped to his knees beside Cassie, barely able to take a breath. Wondering if she was still alive. Both wanting to know and *not* wanting to know at the same time. He reached out to brush her hair from her face. Her eyes were closed. But then her eyelashes fluttered and she opened them.

She was alive. *Thank You, Lord!*

"Hey," Leon said softly, not sure if she realized it was him there beside her. She was gazing forward, not directly at him, and she looked dazed and very pale. "That was quite a landing," he said.

Harry and Martin jogged up, not getting too close, giving them some room.

The light breeze moved Cassie's hair so that it covered her face again. Leon smoothed it once more, this time gently tucking it behind her ear.

Cassie took in a deep, shuddering breath and slowly blew it out. Then she started to turn her face toward Leon.

"Stay still," he said. "Don't move. You might have broken something."

Of course, she ignored him, and continued to very gingerly turn her head.

Leon was a big guy. The years of hard living before he'd gotten his life together showed on his face. He could intimidate men his own size into complying with his directions. But not Cassie. She only listened to him when she felt like it.

"Did you catch them?" she asked. It was evident by the tightness of her voice that she was in pain. And angry.

"I'll catch them later," Leon said. He wouldn't feel a sense of relief until he knew for certain that she was okay.

She started to move, sliding her hands until her palms were flat on the ground and then pushing herself up. Leon wanted to help her, since she seemed so determined, but he was afraid he'd hurt her if he did. She was still wearing her bulletproof vest. Maybe that had helped to protect her spine and her ribs.

Increasingly loud sirens and the growl of a diesel engine announced the arrival of a couple of cop cars and an ambulance. Hopefully, a paramedic would reach Cassie and determine that it was safe for her to move before she pushed herself all the way to her feet.

"The bad guys wore masks again," she said. "I didn't see their faces. Didn't recognize their voices."

"So you're sure they're the same men that shot at us last night?"

She hesitated for a moment. "No, not completely certain."

One very precise and well-planned attempt to kill her, followed by a kidnapping in broad daylight with trash bags used to tie her up. It made no sense.

"I knew you'd find me," Cassie said, looking directly at Leon.

He didn't know how to respond. He was afraid that if he started to tell her the truth—that he would have done anything to find her and make sure she was safe—he would end up telling her too much of what was in his heart. Like how he felt about her. And that would make things awkward between them. So instead he shrugged and said, "Your phone tracker worked."

She let go a short laugh and shook her head slightly. "Yeah, the geniuses grabbed my radio from my hand and never thought to check my pocket for a phone." Her smile faded and her green eyes shone with unshed tears. "They knocked me unconscious, but apparently I wasn't out for very long. I'm pretty sure the plan was to kill me quickly and then dump my body. They just wanted to get far enough away from you and Harry and Martin before they did it so they wouldn't get caught. Then they recognized your truck and knew you were on to them. After that, they heard the police sirens and decided to dump me and run for it."

"Well, you survived," Leon said as two paramedics walked down the hill and approached them. "You're okay." *Thank You, Lord.*

But it had been close. He could have lost her forever. And he and Cassie still had no idea who was trying to kill her.

FIVE

"I have some potential suspect photos for you to look at," Sergeant Bergman said to Cassie in his office.

She sat back in her chair and shook her head. "I won't be of much help. I didn't get a good look at them. They wore masks over their faces."

Cassie and Leon were seated across from the detective's desk in his office at the Stone River Police Department. In the four hours since her kidnapping, Cassie had been checked out by a doctor, who'd confirmed her belief that she hadn't suffered any broken bones. She knew how to fall as safely as possible—thanks to years of horseback riding, hiking and climbing—so she'd tucked her body in when the bad guys had tossed her and she'd rolled down the hill. And the bulletproof vest might have helped.

She was sore. And well aware that the pain would be worse tomorrow. She had some scrapes and a split lip and red marks that would darken into bruises. But she'd survived. And her bounty hunters were all safe. *Thank You, Lord.*

Getting checked out by the doctor had been a top priority. Along with giving the responding officers at the park every shred of information she could think of to track the camper van and catch the kidnappers.

The abandoned van had been located, with the bad guys nowhere in sight. The registered owner was out of town, visiting San Diego with his family, and claimed he had no idea it had been stolen from the side yard of his house.

At the moment, there were no solid leads to follow up on. At least, none that Cassie knew about. Bergman had been out of his office, busy with the investigation of the original attempt on her life, for most of the day. But he'd been contacted by the officers who'd responded to Cassie's abduction.

He'd called her a half hour ago, shortly after he'd returned to department headquarters, asking if she felt up to a meeting. She was still in town, so she'd said yes. Leon had come along with her.

For a moment, her thoughts lingered on Leon and how he'd become such an integral part of her life. No doubt she wouldn't have survived the day if he hadn't responded as quickly and as boldly as he had. Beyond that, he'd become someone she relied on personally. Someone who encouraged her and gave her strength, despite her determination not to let that happen. Not with Leon, an employee. Not with any man, really. Not while her husband's unsolved murder made it so difficult to resolve her grief and return to having a personal life.

Cassie realized she'd been gazing at Leon for a solid minute, maybe more. And that the sergeant was waiting for her to answer his question. Her cheeks burned with embarrassment as she wondered what emotions might have been revealed by the expression on her face as she'd looked at Leon. Fortunately, rather than watching her, Leon appeared to have focused his attention on Bergman along with glancing at the handwritten notes on the detective's desk.

Cassie took a deep breath, refusing to get flustered, as she turned to face Bergman. "I couldn't tell if the two men who attacked me today were the same ones who attacked me last night. Their method of operation this time was very different—much less precise. But that might simply be because they didn't have time to plan ahead. This seemed like an attempt at a quick grab at the first available opportunity. So it could be the same men operating under different circumstances. Or it could be two entirely different assailants." She sighed deeply. "It's hard to accept the idea that two men would fire at my car, cause an accident and try to shoot me in the woods, and then, less than twenty-four hours later, two completely *different* men would kidnap me. But I suppose it's possible."

The detective nodded.

He wasn't going to rule out any possibilities. That was the impression Cassie got from the expression on his face. And Cassie could respect that. Bergman was an independent thinker and fairly methodical, two characteristics that made him good at his job. Jumping to conclusions wasn't really his style.

"Getting back to the photos…" He picked up the tablet sitting on his desk and tapped the screen a few times. "You've already mentioned that the assailants today were wearing masks." He glanced up at Cassie. "Were they wearing glasses, sunglasses, goggles? Anything to cover their eyes?"

"No."

"So you might consider focusing on the subjects' eyes first when you look at these photos. Go through all of them, paying particular attention to the eyes. See if there's anything familiar about them. Then look at them a second time, paying attention to the whole face. If anything triggers even the slightest bit of familiarity, let me know."

"What parameters did you use to select these photos?" Leon asked. "Are they hired muscle? Organized crime?" Cassie had mentioned her theory on a possible organized crime connection to him.

"Just people to consider," Bergman said vaguely. "Think about both attacks on you as you look at them."

Cassie and her bounty hunters had experienced Bergman's polite refusal to share details in an investigation before. There was nothing adversarial about it and she understood why he'd want to keep some things under wraps.

"You might have seen them somewhere without their masks," Bergman said. "When they were planning the attack in the woods, they might have walked by your office window a few times to get an idea of your work routine. Or hung out in a coffee shop you visit fairly regularly. Followed you at court. Something like that.

"They would have wanted to figure out your basic daily pattern and then plan an attack around that. As far as today's abduction goes, that has all the hallmarks of something fairly last minute. Still, they could have been outside your office when you left to go to court. Or in the courthouse parking lot, watching you."

Cassie shivered at the thought of someone stalking her, possibly watching her for days as they plotted to kill her. She was security conscious because of her work, but everything that had happened to her since yesterday evening had taken her thoughts of security to a whole new level. It was a tricky situation. Her job required that she be cautious. But it also required that she shove caution aside when necessary to get the job done.

Bergman got up to hand her the tablet and then sat on the edge of his desk to watch her as she started to flip through the photos. Beside her, Leon leaned in a little closer so that he could see the pictures, too. The light touch of his leg brushing against hers, combined with the overall nearness of him, made her breathe a little more deeply and feel a little more relaxed.

She directed her attention to the pictures, a bit distracted by the exhaustion and body aches starting to settle in. She swiped through the photo lineup several times. But no one looked familiar. She glanced at Leon to see if anyone looked familiar to him. He shook his head. The feeling of disappointment soured her stomach—which was ridiculous. What were the odds of finding the bad guys this quickly and easily?

She handed the tablet back to Bergman, shaking her head. "I'm sorry. No one looks familiar."

"No reason to apologize," Bergman said, setting the tablet on his desk and then walking back around it to sit in his chair. "None of them is a targeted suspect. Just eliminating a few obvious possibilities."

"What about Jerry Lutz?" Leon asked. "The owner of the car found on the fire road near the attack in the woods. You said you were going to go talk to him."

"That is my next topic." Bergman glanced at the paper notepad on his desk. "Lutz still holds a grudge against your late husband," he said to Cassie. "He made that very clear. He still believes that when Jake arrested him, he ruined his life."

Cassie shook her head. The ibuprofen she'd taken earlier had eased her headache a little, but her neck was getting stiff and sore. "If you break the law and you get caught, why is it the officer's fault?"

Bergman raised his brows slightly and gave her a "tell me about it" look, but didn't directly answer the question. "So, Lutz did in fact report that car stolen seven days ago. Well before the attack on you as you crossed the bridge."

Leon made a scoffing sound. "He could have made a false report so he'd have an excuse if his car was seen in the vicinity when the attack happened."

The bounty hunter had leaned close to Cassie while they'd looked at the photos on Bergman's tablet. Even though they were no longer looking at the tablet, Leon still leaned toward Cassie, his leg barely touching hers. And right now, she was being very careful not to make any move that would cause him to lean away from her. His slight touch as he sat beside her, plus his focus on getting information out of the detective and involving himself in the investigation, made her feel taken care of.

She probably shouldn't let herself savor the feeling of being cared for by Leon, but she did. Because she was scared and hurting and she'd been through a lot over the last twenty hours. And, ultimately, what would it hurt? She knew where the solid line was drawn between herself and Leon. An employer on one side and an employee on the other. She knew she wouldn't cross over it.

"I didn't say that Lutz was completely cleared of suspicion," Bergman said evenly. "But I am telling you we have no basis for arresting him. Particularly since he had a very strong alibi for the time of the attack last night that included multiple witnesses."

"What was his alibi?" Cassie asked. She had a vague memory of Lutz from the time Jake was murdered, and she was fairly certain he wasn't one of the abductors today. But what if she was wrong in her belief that the same two men were involved in both attacks on her? Were there actually four men trying to kill her? Could Lutz have been one of the gunmen last night? Or even today? Maybe.

"He likes to throw darts. He's in a competitive league, and he was at the Target Stop throwing darts from four thirty in the afternoon yesterday until shortly after seven in the evening. And during the time of the attack on you today, he was speaking with our officers."

Cassie thought about that for a few seconds. "Do you think somebody is trying to frame him?"

Bergman responded with a slight shrug. "His name was all over the news after Jake was murdered. If a person were looking for someone to frame for an attack on you, anybody with a negative connection to your late husband would be a good candidate. Including Lutz."

"What about Bryan Rogan?" she asked. Earlier, she'd thought he was no longer a viable suspect. But after having more time to mull things over, she'd changed her mind. "What about his loser criminal friends? They wanted to intimidate me into not giving my testimony in court because they knew it could lead to a stronger sentence for Rogan. They obviously didn't stop me. I gave my testimony this morning. But maybe they tried to kill me after the fact because they wanted to punish me. Maybe they wanted to send a message to the other loser criminals about how tough they are."

"It's taking some time to track down all of the different individuals connected to that situation," Bergman said. "But we're working on it. When we find them, we'll see if they have alibis for the window of time when you were abducted today."

"I'd be happy to help you with that," Leon said.

Cassie glanced over at him and saw his jaw muscles tighten.

"My team is handling it," Bergman said. "Remember, just because you only talk to me doesn't mean I'm the only one working the case."

"What's your gut telling you?" Cassie asked. "Is this about my testimony in court? Some fugitive I recovered who's back out of jail and carrying a grudge?" She realized she was talking too fast, thanks to her rattled nerves, so she took a deep breath and blew it out. Maybe, if they could get all of this untangled, they'd finally be able to solve Jake's murder. "Do you think it's related to Jake? Or to the guy in the jail cell who seemed to know something about his murder?"

"That brings us to the last bit of information I have that I can share with you. I've got a name to go with the man in the jail cell with your confidential informant. His name is Seth Tatum."

Cassie felt a flutter in her chest. Maybe this was finally it. The nightmare of Jake's murder would finally be solved.

Bergman tapped his tablet screen a couple of times, then handed the tablet to Cassie to show her Seth Tatum's booking photo. He was a young man, in his early twenties. Which meant he could have been a teenager when Jake was murdered.

"What have you learned from this Seth Tatum?" she asked, hearing her voice tremble a little.

"I'm afraid there's a problem there."

And just like that, Cassie's rising sense of hope turned cold and dropped like a chunk of ice in her stomach. "What do you mean 'problem'?" She handed the tablet back to the sergeant.

"Seth Tatum has vanished. He doesn't answer phone calls. We can't get a location on his cell number, so either he's keeping the phone off and taken out the battery, or he's completely destroyed it. His last known address is over in Montana. We requested help from local law enforcement to check out his residence. He wasn't there. Neighbors say they haven't seen him in several days. His car is parked in his garage."

"So you have no way to locate him," she said dully.

The detective looked her straight in the eyes. "We're not going to give up looking for him just because he isn't easy to find."

"Right." She nodded. And then winced because her neck hurt. "I know that."

Cassie heard some kind of commotion behind her. It was outside Bergman's office, in the open bullpen area of the police station.

Bergman looked past her shoulder toward the noise. As usual, the expression on his face was unreadable. "Have you two been following the local news this afternoon?" he asked.

"I haven't," Cassie said, glancing at Leon.

"Neither have I," Leon looked at the sergeant. "Why?"

Cassie tried to turn to see what was happening behind her, but her hips and legs had grown even more stiff and sore while she'd been sitting in Bergman's office, which made her movements painful and slow. She decided it wasn't worth the effort.

"The attacks on you have made the news, understandably, and drawn a little extra attention from Mayor Al Downing and several of his closest associates on the city council."

"How so?" Cassie asked.

"In covering the story, both local news stations mentioned Jake and the fact that his murder remains unsolved. That got quite a reaction from viewers, with lots of comments on social media. So the reporters have given the cold case some fresh exposure and the mayor has weighed in with comments that he can't believe it's been five years and still no suspects have been brought to justice."

"Is his concern sincere or is this meant to help his next reelection campaign?" Leon asked.

Bergman ignored his question.

"You know what?" Cassie said. "I don't even care. It doesn't matter. If we can find Seth Tatum and develop any leads from the information he has to offer, and the mayor backs a reinvigorated investigation into those leads, including extra funding if necessary, then that's enough for me. If Downing gets some kind of personal, political credit for it—especially if the case is finally solved—I don't care. That's fine."

She'd barely finished her sentence when the sounds behind her became louder and turned from a vague rumble of noise into distinct words.

"I think a quick chat with the lead investigator on the case to get caught up on the details would be warranted," a voice said, and then a familiar-looking man in a navy blue suit stepped into the office. Two other men in suits, who had apparently accompanied him, stayed outside the open door.

"Bergman." The man addressed the detective, who nodded in return.

Mayor Al Downing then turned to Cassie and Leon.

Cassie knew who he was. She'd seen him on TV and around town a few times, but she'd never spoken to him before. He'd been running for his first term when Jake had been murdered, so his election and early days in office were a blur to her.

The mayor introduced himself to Cassie and Leon, shaking hands with each of them, before pulling up a chair and placing it so he could sit by Cassie. "I won't take much of your time," he said. "I just want you to know that everything that's happened to you last night and today has reminded all of us how grateful we are for your late husband's service to our community and the State of Idaho."

"Thank you," Cassie said.

"The city council and I are in unanimous agreement that putting renewed vigor into solving your husband's case and capturing the killer has to be a top priority." He glanced at Bergman. "We'll find a way to free up extra funding to pay for investigators' overtime if need be. This case has remained unsolved for far too long."

Five years, Cassie thought. *Five very long years.*

"I appreciate this," she said.

Maybe the attacks on her, despite how horrible they were, could be turned to good. Maybe this would be what it took to light a fire and get multiple people focused on finding her husband's killer. Sergeant Gabe Bergman was an excellent detective, but he was only one man. And while he had just pointed out that he had other investigators working with him, the fact was the police department still had to budget time and money for investigating current crimes.

Downing had made a decent career for himself arranging funding for businesses in town and especially for property development. That, in turn, had brought in more people, more investors, and more money that had revitalized the former logging town and made it a better place for everyone to live. There were a few naysayers who pointed out that he and his friends had made money off the improvements, too. But at the end of the day, everyone had benefitted. And since he was a man who got things done, maybe Cassie had reason to hope, after all. Despite the fact that they had no solid leads on the attacks on her or on Jake's murder as of the moment.

"You take care of yourself and be careful," the mayor said as he got to his feet. "And if there's anything I can do for you, call my office anytime." He returned his chair, offered a quick goodbye to everyone in the office, and then stepped back out into the bullpen area to rejoin his colleagues. Cassie could hear their voices fading as they walked away.

"Well, that's encouraging," she said, slowly getting to her feet. "And right now I could really use the encouragement."

Leon and Bergman also stood.

"We'll be doing everything we can," Bergman said.

"*Our* first priority will be to remain vigilant," Leon said, looking meaningfully at Cassie. "This renewed focus on Jake's case is a good thing. But it's also stirring up some serious trouble."

He was right. But there was no way Cassie would back down from pursuing justice for her late husband.

Dinner at North Star Ranch that night was subdued with just the ranch residents plus Leon at the table. Leon was fairly certain that Harry and Martin and their wives had been asked to stay away, probably by Adam, so that Cassie could get some rest. Otherwise, they'd be here. Because it was circle-the-wagons time.

Leon was a little surprised that Adam hadn't reacted more strongly to the attack on Cassie earlier in the day when he'd rushed to the urgent care medical facility to see for himself what kind of shape she was in. But Adam did have decades of experience in keeping himself and other people calm in harrowing situations. If it weren't for the rheumatoid arthritis issues he'd developed, he would probably still be running the daily operation of Rock Solid Bail Bonds himself instead of handing it over to his daughter. From what Leon could see, the medicines and therapies Adam took helped much of the time. But some days were obviously rough for him.

Leon sat at the dining room table beside Cassie, having already quickly cleaned his plate. He hadn't realized how long he'd gone without eating until he and Cassie had walked through the door and the mouthwatering scent of meat loaf glazed with barbecue sauce had practically assaulted him. Sherry and Jay had hugged Cassie and asked her how she was holding up. They hadn't gone overboard with their concern, which Cassie appeared to appreciate.

"I might need you to hang out at the downtown office for the next few days," Cassie said to her dad after setting her utensils on her empty plate when she was finished eating and sitting back in her chair.

Leon was glad to see she had a healthy appetite even after all she'd been through.

"So, you're going to stay home and rest for a few days," Adam said. "That's a good idea."

"Actually, Dad, I need you to take care of business while I focus on Jake's case."

"What exactly do you plan to do?" Leon interjected himself into the father-daughter conversation. He'd already guessed that she was going to turn her full attention on finding Jake's killer. And wherever Cassie was going, Leon was going, too.

She glanced over at him, eyebrows raised, a defensive look on her face. But then her expression began to soften. "How long has it been since you've gotten some sleep?" she asked.

"I don't know," Leon said dismissively. *About thirty-four hours.* He ran his hand over his jaw.

"Why don't you go home? Get some rest."

"I am going home in a few minutes. To grab some clothes and then come right back. I'm here for the duration."

Cassie's eyes got shiny. She sniffed and looked away.

"You really ought to stay here at the house and rest a few days," Adam muttered looking at Cassie. "But I understand how badly you want to find the lowlife who murdered Jake. And this does feel like the time to move on whatever lead you've got before it vanishes."

Spoken like a true bounty hunter.

Cassie turned to her dad. "Thank you."

"But I also think pushing this investigation could get you killed." Adam turned a steely gaze to Leon. "You're welcome to stay here while all of this is going on. In fact, I want you to. These thugs may end up coming to the ranch to try to get to Cassie. I want you to make sure you've got her back *all* the time."

Leon nodded. "Yes, sir."

Cassie stood, moving slowly, and then picked up her plate.

From across the table, Sherry waved at her to put the plate down. "Don't worry about that. Jay and I can clear the table. You go on to your room and get some rest."

"I will eventually," Cassie said. "Right now I've got some things to research."

She started walking stiffly toward the office and Leon got up and followed her. "Can't this wait until morning?" he asked when she sat in front of her laptop. "Your brain will be fresher and sharper."

She exhaled deeply. "I know. I just want to do a little research on Seth Tatum."

Leon pulled up a chair to sit beside her and watched as the search results didn't bring up much information about Seth.

"No social media accounts," she muttered. "A couple of general information listings establishing that he resides in Saddleback, Montana. Or at least he has until recently." She tried an image search, but didn't find anything. Even the booking photo Bergman showed her hadn't been publicly posted yet.

"Well, if we have to track down a guy with almost no information to begin with, it won't be the first time," Leon said.

Cassie nodded, leaning away from the computer screen and then slowly standing. "I wouldn't be alive if it weren't for you," she said softly. "And I wouldn't be able to do this investigation without you."

For what seemed like the millionth time, Leon felt the tug to reach out and wrap his arms around her. But if he did, he would pull her too tightly to his chest and hold her for too long.

"Go to sleep," he said, refusing to give in to the tempting tenderness of the moment. "I'm going to run home, then I'll come back here and catch some sleep, too."

He needed to get out, get some fresh air, put some distance between them.

He *had* to stay sharp. Because while Cassie focused on finding whoever killed her husband, Leon needed to be on the lookout for whoever was intent on killing Cassie.

SIX

At noon the next day—a Saturday with good weather at the start of tourist season—there were plenty of people milling around on Main Street in Stone River. They filled up the sidewalk tables outside the small restaurants and coffee shops, and the crowded conditions made it easier for Cassie and Leon to thread their way through downtown to find the people they wanted to talk to without drawing too much attention to themselves.

In particular, they were looking to talk to former clients. A few of the people in need of the services provided by Rock Solid Bail Bonds were criminals by choice. Some were people who'd had a bad day. Many were people struggling in their battle with addiction, and due to a moment in time when their addiction had had the upper hand, they'd needed a bail bondswoman.

Some were actually innocent of the criminal charges they were facing.

At the end of the day, a fair number were ultimately decent people who didn't want to see the world break down into chaos. So they'd been willing to supply Cassie with information when she needed it.

"Have you overheard anyone talking about the attacks on me?" Cassie asked Krystal, a former client who was working the bar at the lakeside Bellport Inn.

The French doors facing Lake Bell in the café section of the inn were open, providing a wide view of the deep mountain lake on the other side of the narrow street, the jagged mountains in the distance and the bright blue sky above.

The bar was relatively quiet, the lunch crowd mostly opting for nonalcoholic drinks. At night, especially on the weekends, the bar would be packed. The café had a relaxed atmosphere and it was located near the downtown hub of fun, drawing in locals despite the tourist crowds in the summer months. It wasn't unusual for Krystal to see a bail jumper Cassie was looking for or to occasionally overhear a bit of useful information.

Krystal was in her early twenties with wide blue eyes, a blond ponytail and multiple glittering stud earrings in each ear. "Cassie, when I heard about the attack on you over by the Shackleford Inlet I was so worried. And then I heard about you getting kidnapped." She shook her head sympathetically. "I'm so glad to see that you're okay." Krystal leaned a little closer and dropped her voice. "And the bruises on your face aren't really all that noticeable. The makeup covers them pretty well."

Yeah, well, even if they didn't look bad, they *felt* bad. Nearly every part of her body hurt. Maybe it would have been wise for Cassie to stay home and recuperate for a few days. But the reality was that something was going on related to Jake's murder. She felt certain of it even if she didn't have the facts to prove it yet. Staying home and letting time pass could end with the trail growing cold. She'd waited for this break too long to let it slip away.

Plus, if she hunkered down and hid, that might only make the attackers bolder. Yes, the police were on the job investigating and looking for the bad guys. And she was grateful. But the bad guys were after *her* personally, and the best thing she could do was push back however she could and throw them off balance.

Cassie nodded. "Thank you for your concern, but I'm fine."

"I haven't heard anything useful. I'm sorry," Krystal said after refilling a couple of glasses with ice and cola for a busy waitress.

"What exactly have you heard?" Cassie asked. Krystal's assessment of what was useful could be mistaken. Cassie's job was all about following up on small, seemingly inconsequential details.

"I've overheard people last night and the night before talking about the attacks since the local news had reported it. Just general chatter. How awful it was. What's the world come to? That kind of thing."

"Did you hear the name Jake Hollister mentioned?" Leon asked from behind Cassie. He'd made himself a kind of human backstop everywhere the two of them had gone in town. Whether he thought Cassie might topple over at any minute and he needed to be there to catch her, or he intended to place himself as a barrier between her and anyone who might attack her, she wasn't sure.

Krystal glanced at Leon, and Cassie could see the expression in the young woman's blue eyes appear to shutter. It could mean she was about to give an answer that wasn't entirely forthcoming. But it could also mean that she was intimidated by having Leon speak directly to her. He was a large guy who looked like bad news. That sometimes came in handy. But not always.

"I don't remember hearing that name mentioned specifically by a patron." Krystal shifted her gaze back to Cassie. "The mayor was on the TV over the bar, talking about what happened to you. And to your husband. How the person who killed him still needs to be found. I heard a few people talk about that." She shrugged.

"Well, that's good," Cassie said, thinking out loud and responding to Krystal at the same time. "People are paying attention. Maybe making it more than a news story that's here today and forgotten tomorrow." She glanced over her shoulder at Leon. "It means an added layer of pressure on the bad guys." She cocked an eyebrow. "Maybe they'll get impatient and sloppy."

He nodded.

"Thanks," Cassie said to Krystal.

They walked outside, weaving between the strolling tourists on the sidewalk, eventually turning a corner that took them away from the area near the lakefront park and back toward the center of town.

"You realize this 'added pressure' on the bad guys means more danger for you, right?" Leon said once they were clear of the foot traffic and could walk side by side.

Cassie laughed and shook her head, thinking of the expression on his face while she'd talked to Krystal. "You were just dying to say something to me, weren't you?"

"This is taking on the feel of something much bigger than our usual bounty hunts." His voice sounded weighted with concern. "I know we've faced dangerous people before. But at least then we had arrest and bail bond records. Police records or information from other bond agencies asking for your help. *Something.* We knew for the most part who and what we were looking for. But with these attacks…" He shook his head. "We've got no clue."

"But we'll have a clue, soon, after either Bergman tracks down Seth Tatum or we do, and we find out why he was passing through Stone River and what he knows about Jake's murder." Cassie offered her best reassuring smile to Leon because she knew what it was like to worry for someone else's safety. Night before last, in the forest, she'd also been *very* worried for Leon. But at the moment, her thoughts were focused on finding Jake's killer. And she was confident she was doing everything she could to keep Leon and herself safe.

"You sound certain this Seth guy will be found alive," Leon said.

"Well, I try to be optimistic." She'd considered the possibility that even the cops couldn't find Seth Tatum because he was dead. But dwelling on that wouldn't get her anywhere. So she'd decided to assume he was alive until she knew otherwise. And she'd decided not to ask Krystal or any of her other informants if they recognized Seth's name. Cassie didn't want Seth to know she was looking for him. And she didn't want to unintentionally send bad guys after him. Until she better understood what she was dealing with when it came to Seth, she needed to be very careful.

They continued walking toward a section of town with industrial businesses, including a repair shop for boat bodies and engines. That business had an employee Cassie wanted to speak with. Jimmy Moreno had once been picked up for residential burglary and his family had gone to Rock Solid Bail Bonds to get him out of lockup. The charges had eventually been dropped. Maybe he'd been innocent. Maybe he'd gotten away with a crime. In any event, he had friends who'd been arrested on multiple occasions. Cassie suspected he knew more about the criminal activities around Stone River than the average person, so she figured she'd show up at his workplace to ask if he'd heard anything about the attacks on her or maybe even Jake's murder.

Unfortunately, as soon as she found him in the cavernous repair shop, he made it clear that he had nothing to say to her. And he punctuated that point by dropping his welding mask over his face and getting right back to work.

"Well, that was a bust," she said to Leon as the two of them walked out of the shop and into the bright sunlight.

"Maybe not," Leon said slowly.

Cassie glanced over at him and then followed his gaze. A familiar figure had stepped out from the narrow alley between two buildings and onto the sidewalk, where he hesitated.

"Is that Phil Warner?" Leon asked.

"Sure looks like him." After telling Cassie about his cellmate who'd ultimately been identified as Seth Tatum, the informant had done a disappearing act. She'd called and texted him multiple times, wanting to revisit every single detail that Phil could remember regarding his time spent with Seth. But Phil, who was normally quick to respond to an opportunity to earn a few easy bucks by sharing information, had not replied. Stopping by his downtown apartment later today to look for him was already on Cassie's to-do list.

Phil started moving down the sidewalk then paused in front of a tavern.

Cassie and Leon followed him.

"Phil!" Cassie called out as he reached for the tavern door.

He turned and, as they closed in on him, she could see his eyes grow rounder. He yanked the door open and ran inside.

"I'll head for the back," Leon said, sprinting for the narrow alley on the other side of the tavern.

Cassie raced for the front door, grimacing at the pain emanating from her sore muscles.

The dark tavern's interior was jarring after the bright sunlight. The glow from the neon beer signs and the TV over the bar showing a baseball game gave off just enough light for her to see where she was going.

She spotted six people seated at the bar and about the same number at surrounding tables. She'd have to get closer to each of them in this dim light to figure out if one of them might be Phil. Because now, after he'd seen her and bolted, she was determined to find out why he was hiding from her.

A flash of bright sunlight blinded her for a second. Someone had opened the back door. She saw a silhouette that fit the size and shape of Phil. And then she saw another, much larger, silhouette step into the frame created by the doorway. Leon. Cassie hurried toward the back as Phil retreated into the tavern and Leon let the door drop shut behind him.

"What's the matter, Phil?" Cassie asked. "You not in the mood for a chat?"

"Looks to me like he was more in the mood to skedaddle," Leon said after a few seconds passed and the informant hadn't responded. He turned to Phil. "You got someplace you need to be?"

Phil's slight build and big brown eyes made him appear younger than his thirty-five years at first glance. But this close, even in the dim light, Cassie could see the lines marking the passage of time on his face. She could also see the fear in his eyes.

Phil lifted his chin defiantly. "You can't stop me from leaving if I want to. I'm no bail jumper and you two aren't cops."

"We wouldn't dream of stopping you." Cassie glanced at Leon and he took a step aside so that he was no longer physically blocking Phil from the exit. "I just wanted a minute to talk." She reached into her jeans' pocket for the cash she always kept on hand for moments like this, when a small incentive might make a situation run smoother.

Phil reached for the money and she yanked it back. "We talk first."

She moved to a nearby plastic-topped rickety table and sat on a chair, stifling the slight moan triggered by her sore hip. Phil dropped down in the chair across from her while Leon grabbed a chair from a nearby table and brought it over for himself.

"Why have you been hiding from me?" Cassie asked. "You didn't return my calls or texts. You ran when I called out to you. What's going on?"

"Nothing." Phil wiped his forehead with the back of his hand. "I just wasn't in the mood to talk to you." He sat straighter in the chair and squared his shoulders. "I wanted to be left alone."

"You're afraid," Cassie said. "It's obvious. Tell me

why. Did someone threaten you? Did Seth Tatum threaten you?"

"Who?"

The confusion on Phil's face appeared genuine. Cassie knew that he was a smooth liar but not a particularly good actor.

"Seth Tatum," Cassie said. "That's the name of the guy in the jail cell you told me about."

"Oh," Phil said, his eyebrows vaulting slightly, as though that were an interesting bit of information. "He never told me his name. Or if he did, I forgot it."

"Is anybody threatening you?" Cassie asked. "Because Leon and I might be able to help you if they are."

Phil glanced at Leon. Leon nodded in return. Phil looked uncertain about the situation.

"Nobody threatened me, Cassie," Phil finally said, dropping his hands from the tabletop to his lap. "But I've heard about the attacks on you. I'm glad you're okay."

"Thank you."

He tilted his head slightly and broke eye contact with her, shifting his gaze to his hands in his lap. "When I heard about the people coming after you, maybe even trying to kill you, I got scared. I thought it might have something to do with what I told you. And then I saw on TV that the mayor was looking into ramping up the investigation into your husband's murder. After that, I got really scared that whoever killed your husband would find out what I told you and they'd come after me."

"I can understand you being worried, but I doubt you're on anybody's radar," Cassie said. "I think you're safe talking to me. So tell me, what did you and Seth talk about while you were locked up together?"

Phil shook his head. "I already told you everything

I remember, which isn't much. I'd been drinking. I was starting to sober up when he began crying and babbling about something. I had a splitting headache and I wasn't in the mood to listen to him. I just remember him saying that he knew something about the murder of a state trooper who lived in Stone River."

Sometimes a person could mention Jake's murder and Cassie would feel a familiar wave of sadness. Other times, like now, it triggered a sharp stab of grief in the center of her chest. She took a deep breath and forced the feeling aside.

"Did you come here to meet someone?" Cassie asked, glancing past Phil's shoulder.

Phil shook his head. "Nah, I just came here for lunch. When the game is on, you can get two hot dogs for a dollar."

Cassie handed the cash still in her hand across the table to Phil. "Here, why don't you go get lunch at a place with better food?"

His eyes lit up. "I will!" He snatched the money from her hand. "Thanks. We're done here, right?"

Cassie nodded and Phil didn't waste any time getting up and heading out the back door.

"I could go for some lunch," Leon said. "How about you?"

"I could eat. But not here."

"No, not here."

They headed for the front door. It felt to Cassie like every eye on the place was on them. She might just be paranoid. But she had good reason to be.

"I don't think Stefan Kasparov had a clue that some joint drug task force was watching him five years ago.

Much less that he would have targeted that cop who got murdered." Travis Jefferson, small-time intermittent drug dealer, rubbed a hand through his bristly red hair and spared a glance toward Cassie.

Leon could see the guy's freckled face turn a little redder. He'd probably just remembered *that cop who got murdered* had been Cassie's husband.

"Sorry," Travis muttered before looking away from her.

It was early evening and the three of them were standing outside the bodega where Travis worked while he took his break and smoked a cigarette. Scents from a burger stand down the street drifted in their direction and Leon's stomach rumbled. He'd long ago burned through his fish taco lunch with Cassie and now he was hungry for dinner. Fortunately, Travis was the last person on their list to be interviewed today.

They had tried a slightly different tactic when questioning this afternoon, asking specifically if the informant or client had heard anything about three particular people. Bryan Rogan, whose trial should conclude in the upcoming week. Jerry Lutz, who apparently still blamed Jake for his wife's leaving him after he'd gone to prison. And even Stefan Kasparov, the drug supplier the joint-agency law enforcement task force had been focused on when Jake was murdered.

Travis Jefferson was the fifth person they'd talked to since lunch. They'd gotten some interesting general information so far, but nothing that could direct them to the killer. That was okay, though. They'd made it clear they would pay for information, which meant any one of the people they'd talked to might now go in search of good information in exchange for cash.

So far, Travis was the only person willing to say anything at all about Kasparov. The others had seemed afraid to even say his name. He was known to be a very violent man.

"I'm surprised to hear that you think Stefan had no clue he was being watched by the task force," Cassie said to Travis. "Clearly, he's a sharp guy. He's still in business, managing to stay out of lockup for the last five years despite supplying massive amounts of drugs to the region."

Travis shrugged. "Five years ago, Stefan knew he was smart and I'd venture to guess he was sure he was smarter than the cops. He wasn't looking over his shoulder as much as he should have been. Then the state trooper was killed. After that, Stefan got hauled in for questioning. He was a suspect for a while. He wised up after that and got more secretive. But until that point, he didn't have the motivation to go after any cop. He didn't think they were a threat to him."

Leon glanced over at Cassie. She gave him a quick nod, which told him she believed what Travis was telling her and that she was finished talking with him.

Leon reached into his pocket for some money to pay for the information. He'd recovered Travis a couple of different times after he'd been absent for court dates related to drug possession charges and his bond had been revoked. He was nearing thirty years old, generally polite, and the assessment he'd just given Cassie of Stefan Kasparov seemed like the truth.

After thanking him and saying their goodbyes, Leon and Cassie walked to Leon's truck. Once they were inside, he cranked up the engine and headed for the historic downtown area and the Rock Solid Bail Bonds office.

Cassie was quiet as they drove along the narrow streets. Leon noticed she was watching the side mirror to make sure they weren't being followed. He was likewise keeping an eye out for anyone tailing them.

"You must be worn out after all you've been through with the attacks and then hiking around town all day."

She didn't respond at first. He glanced over and saw that she had shifted her attention to Lake Bell and the lights along the shoreline that appeared to flicker in the purple evening glow.

"Talking about Jake really brings it all back," she said without facing him, her voice scratchy with emotion. "Some days it feels like he's been gone a million years, and other days it feels like he was here just a few minutes ago."

The sorrowful tone of her voice hit Leon square in the center of his chest. He desperately wanted to do something to make things better for her, but there was nothing he could do. The man she had loved had been taken from her. Brutally murdered. Leon didn't know what to say. He'd been through some tough times, but nothing quite like that.

"I'm sorry," he finally said.

They stopped at a red light. She sighed deeply. When she exhaled, he could see her tense shoulders drop noticeably. She turned to him. "I just feel so stuck," she said. "Jake has passed on. I accept that. I have for a while, truly. But I'm still here and I can't seem to get moving again with my life. Work is fine. But my life feels stuck."

This was Cassie letting down a major emotional wall in front of Leon. Not something she normally did.

Maybe not something she *ever* did. Cassie Wheeler was a physically small woman with a sterling reputation in a tough and oftentimes dangerous profession. Being vulnerable was never part of her game plan. Leon felt honored and terrified at the same time. What could he possibly do to make things better for her? What could he say?

Dear Lord, please give me the right words, he prayed silently.

The light turned green and they moved forward through the intersection.

"Sometimes being frustrated is a good sign," he said, deciding just to go with what he honestly thought rather than try to be wise or clever. He considered the stretch of time in his own life when he'd felt stuck. When his own battles with alcohol, with drugs and with stupid behavior got him locked up a few times. Finally, frustration had pushed him to seek something more for his life. And faith had become his answer. He knew that faith was a firm foundation in Cassie's life, too.

"If you want to move forward, you have to get used to not knowing exactly what the next step is going to be," he said. "At least, that was my experience. And that's hard for people like you and me, because we know how much danger there is in the world. But sometimes staying still isn't the best answer. And so you've got to take a risk and make that first small move."

Was she intimating what he'd thought she was when she'd said her life felt stuck? That she was looking for romance? That meant she'd be moving toward building a relationship with a new man in her life. It made Leon feel hollow just thinking about it. But he wanted her to be happy. And her happiness was more important to him than any pity party he might hold for himself the first time he saw her with another man.

Cassie didn't say anything for the rest of the drive and Leon was honestly relieved. He was already worried that he'd said the wrong thing. He wasn't exactly a life coach kind of guy.

He pulled into a slot in the parking area behind the Rock Solid Bail Bonds office.

"You know what?" Cassie asked just before he cut the engine.

"What?"

"You're a lot smarter than you look."

A laugh came out of Leon that arose from the depths of his belly, breaking the tension he'd felt for the last few minutes. It was a reassurance that the connection between the two of them was still there. At least for now.

"Why, thank you, ma'am," he replied.

She moved slowly as she got out of the truck.

"We're heading out to the ranch in a half hour," he announced just before she unlocked the back door of the office and disabled the alarm. "If there's still work that needs to be done beyond that time that you can't take care of at the ranch, then we'll get Harry or Martin and Daisy to come down here and deal with it."

"I mainly just wanted to grab the mail," she said, walking toward the front door where a few envelopes had been pushed in through the narrow slot and had piled on the floor. "And since we're here, I might as well check the phone for messages."

Leon had locked the back door behind him and was heading into the main office when he heard the sound of shattering glass. They'd had rocks and bricks thrown through the window before. It was the nature of their business that people got upset by the work that they did. Still, a rock or brick to the head could be lethal. It was definitely something to take seriously.

He raced forward and saw the hole in the plate-glass window. Then he spotted Cassie, apparently unscathed, looking at the floor. He was just rounding a desk to see what she was looking at when a second object crashed through the window.

That object landed on the floor and rolled to a stop. Metal. Cylindrical. Something attached to the end. Like maybe a detonator.

"Bomb!" he yelled, grabbing Cassie and half dragging, half carrying her as he raced for the rear exit. He had to get them both outside before the devices exploded. His fingers fumbled with the multiple latches as he desperately tried to get her out of there in time.

But he was too late.

SEVEN

Leon threw himself on top of Cassie as the first blast rocketed through the office. The sudden loud bang was followed by a rush of hot, pressurized air that flung broken glass, shards of ripped wood and plastic, and bits of metal through the air. The fiery whirlwind felt like a burning, cutting cloud as it made its way over Leon's body and the protective cage he'd formed around Cassie's head with his bent arms.

She felt a little nauseated in the aftermath and her head was swimming.

Seconds after the pressure wave passed, she tried to move. Leon's body was like a deadweight on top of her. Something terrible had happened to him. She knew it. With a feeling of sickening dread in the pit of her stomach, she tried to place the palms of her hands flat on the floor beneath her shoulders so she could push herself up. But she couldn't budge. He was way too heavy.

Bang! Another explosion brought a fresh wave of heat and deepened her fear for Leon, who was still unmoving. How many more of these blasts would there be? And then she remembered—there were two explosive devices thrown through the window. This second one didn't sound as loud as the first, and the rush of air and debris didn't seem as direct. This bomb must have been the one that had rolled toward the other side of the office, away from the area where she and Leon now lay on the ground.

Fine bits of plaster particles floated down around them.

"Hey, are you okay?" she called out to Leon, painfully aware that he had taken the brunt of the blast to protect her.

He finally began to stir, lifting his arms from her head and then shifting his weight and moving away from her.

He was alive. *Thank You, Lord.*

Now, she could push herself up. As she did, Leon took hold of her upper arms and helped her into a sitting position. "Are you all right?" he asked.

She nodded. "Yes. How about you?"

"I'm fine."

He was dusted with the debris from the explosion. They were in the short hallway by the back door. Fortunately, the adjoining small office that served as a break room and kitchen had apparently absorbed a significant amount of the impact from the blasts.

Cassie looked around dazedly. The electricity had been knocked out. And yet there was light.

She smelled something burning. And then she saw the smoke, black and billowing, and rapidly growing in intensity. It crossed the reception area and curled around in the direction of her and Leon, moving as though it were some dark, glowing creature trying to seek them out.

The overhead sprinklers kicked on, but weren't

spraying water fast enough to get ahead of the increasing flames. The fire extinguishers they kept on hand were clearly too small to bring the quickly increasing conflagration under control.

Her office, filled with mementos and pictures, was being destroyed right in front of her. She was horrified to watch it happen, and yet she couldn't look away. Despite the water spraying from the ceiling, the glow was turning brighter and the fire was getting bigger. Cassie stared at the flames, transfixed, trying to make sense of what had just happened and what was still happening. Maybe the explosives contained their own fuel. Maybe one or both had landed in just the right spot where there was already fuel in place to feed the resulting flames.

Leon pulled her to her feet and in the direction of the back door. Behind her, she could hear cracking and popping, and the sounds of wood paneling and shelves breaking and collapsing. But she also felt Leon close by. He had her back, like he always did, and that was a good thing, because her brain didn't seem particularly sharp at the moment. Maybe she'd hit her head when he'd shoved her to the ground. She couldn't quite remember. Maybe she'd just hit her head one too many times during the course of the attacks over the last few days.

"I should try to save as much as I can," Cassie shouted over the noise of the fire and collapsing debris, her thoughts shifting to the pictures on the walls. Many were from the pre-digital age and no copies existed. Some were from the very early years of the business, and included images of Cassie's late mother back when she was young. From the glow, it looked like the fire was centered at one end of the office. If she hurried, she might be able to grab something close by. She started to turn.

"No!" Leon shouted. "We've got to get out!"

He was right, of course.

Leon unfastened the last of the latches on the back door and yanked it open, stepping aside so Cassie could go first.

The burst of cool, clean air instantly revived her, though she also knew the rush of oxygen would feed the fire burning in the office. She stepped up to the threshold and heard sounds from the parking lot that she couldn't quite identify over the growing roar of the fire behind her. And then she saw the splintered gouges suddenly appearing on the door frame to the right of her. Bullet holes. Someone was *shooting* at her. *"Gun!"*

She jammed her body backward, pushing into Leon as she quickly slammed the thick door shut and bolted it. Her body began to shake. Whether it was from fear or fatigue or heightened levels of adrenaline racing through her, she didn't know. And it didn't matter.

Get it together, she snapped to herself.

More bullets hit the door, one blasting all the way through and striking the floor near Cassie's foot. Once the shooter got close enough, more bullets would penetrate the door. She and Leon retreated farther into the office, where the smoke was now thicker and the temperature hotter.

There was an odd creaking sound as a heavy wrought-iron light fixture, anchored to an exposed wooden beam in the ceiling above the main area of the office, began to pull away from its base. It crashed to the floor, sending out a spray of glass and stirring up a flare of cinders as it rolled toward the front door.

"We've got to get out of here *now*!" Leon shouted near her ear.

With the heated metal light fixture blocking the door, they were going to have to get out through the broken window. The thick smoke and noise from the fire and all of the objects breaking and collapsing around them made it impossible for Cassie to see or to hear if emergency services responders were outside the office yet.

Leon grabbed the coat tree near the door. He pulled off the sweater that was on it and tossed it to Cassie. "Hold that."

She caught the sweater and held it, watching as he jabbed the tip of the coat tree toward one of the areas where the glass was already broken. He used it to clear away some of the deadly pointed shards.

Despite all the noise, Cassie could still hear shots being fired at the locked back door. The trap that had been set up was horrific and smart. They had been boxed in by fire in the front of the building and a shooter at the back.

Could there be *another* shooter waiting for them outside the front of the building, as well?

"What if they're out front, too, waiting to shoot us?" she called to Leon. The smoke made her cough, the scent of charred wood giving her a horrible headache.

Leon paused for a second. After a few more jabs with the coat tree, he finished clearing the window. Then he turned to Cassie and gestured for the sweater.

She tossed it to him.

"Get your gun," he said, after laying the sweater across the bottom of the window frame to cover the few remaining jagged tips of glass.

She pulled her pistol out of her waistband. Cassie

did not normally walk around town with a gun. But considering everything that had happened lately, she'd carried one with her all day today.

"I'm going through the window first," Leon said. "You cover me. If anybody starts shooting at me, you shoot back."

Cassie shook her head and rubbed at her burning, watering eyes. What if someone out there started taking shots at Leon and she was unable to stop them because she couldn't see well enough to shoot? The toughest part of her job was not facing fear for herself. Even though she did fear for her own safety at times. Being responsible for someone else's safety was *the most* stressful consideration she faced in her line of work. As the owner of Rock Solid Bail Bonds, she held a position of trust and responsibility. And she wasn't about to pass a dangerous action on to someone else to carry it out.

"I'll go out first," she said loudly. She'd rather put him in the position of having to breathe smoke for a few extra seconds than risk having him shot as the first person out of the building.

Her attempt to physically elbow Leon aside didn't get her anywhere.

"I've got it under control," he said.

If this weren't a life and death situation, she would have argued with him. Instead, she blinked rapidly several times and rubbed her eyes with the heel of her free hand, trying to clear her vision as much as possible in case she had to return fire at a lurking shooter.

Meanwhile, Leon crouched and threw one leg through the opening in the window. He steadied himself and then brought the other leg through so that he was finally outside. Cassie kept her gun ready to fire, heart rising into her throat, terrified that something bad would happen to him.

Smoke was already rolling out of the broken window. Now it was beginning to thin just enough that she could see Leon on the sidewalk outside, red and blue flashing lights just beyond him.

The police presence should mean the scene was secure. The shooting at the back door had stopped. But considering all that had happened over the last few days, Cassie didn't dare let her guard down. Instead, she focused her attention, willing herself to see through the smoky haze to make certain no one was out there waiting to take a shot at Leon.

"Cassie!" Leon's voice startled her. "I think we're good out here." He stood on the other side of the busted-out window, stretching his hands toward her.

Behind him, in the drifting smoke, she saw a fire engine and a couple of firefighters jumping off the emergency rig, grabbing heavy hoses and hurrying toward the burning office.

Finally convinced that it was safe, Cassie tucked her gun into her waistband. She reached for Leon's hand as she climbed out through the window. Instead of taking her hand, Leon grasped her upper arms, keeping a solid hold on her as she moved through the frame and onto the sidewalk.

A police officer rushed toward them. On the street behind him, an ambulance rolled up.

"We're okay," Cassie said to the officer. "There's no one else in the office."

"Let's get you away from here," the cop said. He motioned Cassie and Leon closer to the street, which was quickly being blocked by arriving emergency vehicles.

"Someone threw two pipe bombs through the front window," Cassie said to the cop. "And there was a shooter in the back parking lot."

The officer nodded. "We're already checking on the parking lot situation. We got several calls reporting two explosions and gunfire."

Cassie let out a laugh that was nearly a sob. "I'm glad somebody called. I didn't even have time to think of grabbing my phone. I just wanted to get out before everything collapsed around us."

Firefighters aimed their hoses and began targeting the office with streams of water. The remaining glass in the front windows shattered, and the carved wooden Rock Solid Bail Bonds sign that hung on the outside of the building crashed onto the sidewalk, breaking into several pieces.

Cassie stood and stared at her office, seeing the destruction in front of her and also seeing the memories flickering through her mind. Good times spent with her mom and dad. With Jake. With her bounty hunters.

Beside her, Leon wrapped an arm around her shoulder and she leaned into him.

Every day she tried very hard to remember to count her blessings. But there were times like this, when it felt like too many things that she cared about had been taken away, that her heart could not withstand any more sorrow.

Leon stood at the open door of the ambulance looking at Cassie, who was seated inside on a narrow, padded bench. The paramedic who'd been checking on her leaned back, pulled the ear pieces of her stethoscope out of her ears and said, "Your heart sounds strong. But your lungs sound a little raspy, and I've obviously heard you cough a few times. You might consider going to the hospital to get that checked out."

Cassie shook her head. "I'm fine. And, honestly, while some of my coughing is from the smoke, I think a lot of it is from the dust floating around after the explosions. Thank you." She started to stand, moving slowly and stiffly, Leon noted, and the medic moved out of the way.

"Your turn," the paramedic said to Leon as Cassie stepped out of the ambulance.

Leon shook his head. "I'm fine." None of his bones were broken. The back of his neck felt like it was sun-burned, likely due to the heat of the explosions, but it was something he could live with. His smoke-irritated lungs were feeling better with each breath of cool night-time mountain air that he drew in. And the small cuts on his skin from the flying debris were nothing.

None of it mattered, anyway. Because there was no way he was going to climb into the back of the ambulance while Cassie stood outside it. She'd potentially be a target if the shooters were still in the neighborhood. It didn't matter how many cops and emergency workers milled around—and there were plenty. He wasn't leaving her side.

Cassie stared at him and he could tell by the look in her eyes that she was irritated with his decision. He could also tell by the drooping of her shoulders and the slack expression on her face that she was too tired to argue.

She'd been through so much in the last few days. So much in the last few years, really, with her husband's unsolved murder hanging over her head. And still she kept going. He admired and respected that. At the same time, he wanted to help hold her up. Carry some of the burden for her. He couldn't bring her husband back to life. Couldn't ease that heartache over her loss. God would have to do the heavy lifting when it came to that. But he could do some of the small things. Like watch her back—especially when someone was clearly determined to kill her. And he could keep doing that even when it annoyed her.

She finally turned away from him to look at the Rock Solid Bail Bonds office. The flames had been knocked out. The three fire engines' giant floodlights shone on the building, making visible the light layer of smoke still roiling out as they sprayed water on it. Electricity to the surrounding buildings had been temporarily shut off to avoid the threat of electrocution. Several firefighters were standing by with rakes to go inside and stir up hot spots to ensure the fire was completely out.

"Well, I see you two are still alive."

Leon turned at the sound of Sergeant Bergman's voice as the detective approached them. Normally, Bergman was the picture of professionalism and always dressed in a suit and tie. But right now he was wearing jeans, cowboy boots, an untucked shirt and a leather jacket. It made the lawman look younger than he usually did, and almost like a regular guy instead of a cop.

"Sorry to be the reason you got called into work on what was obviously your day off," Cassie said.

"Are you kidding?" the detective responded. "This is what I live for."

Bergman didn't crack a smile and Leon couldn't tell if he was being dry-humored or serious.

"I've already been briefed by the initial responding officers," Bergman said, holding up a notepad Leon hadn't noticed until now. "They told me about the incendiary devices, so I've contacted the Feds for help on that. They might recognize the work and have suggestions on who made them. At the least, they'll be able to tell us about the skills it took to make them, who might have those sorts of skills, what ingredients they needed, where they might have procured them, that sort of thing. And there's a good chance they'll offer us assistance on the investigation."

"Somebody on the street had to have seen something," Cassie said. "Even with it being a Saturday evening and many of the businesses in this part of town closed, there's still always *some* traffic around here. People going to and from the police department headquarters, if nothing else. And then there was the shooter at the back door. Someone must have seen something helpful there, too."

"We're all over *all* of this," Bergman said. "Surveying the crime scene. Canvassing the area and talking to people. Contacting business owners and requesting security video. We know how to do our jobs."

"Right." Cassie nodded. "Of course you do."

"Did you get any warning this was going to happen?" Bergman asked. "Anybody threaten to do something like this? I want you to think about everybody you deal with. Not just the attacks on you over the last few days."

Cassie shook her head. "No. No warning. No threats."

"Do either of you know anyone with the skills to make bombs?" Bergman turned to Leon. "You were in the building. You could have been the target of this attack."

Leon thought about that. "I know a few people who might dream of doing something like this. But to actually carry it out?" He shook his head. "No one comes to mind. I haven't had a big falling out with anyone lately.

I couldn't tell you if any of my enemies have bomb-making skills." He shrugged. "I've heard you can find the directions to make an explosive online, so I guess anyone who is determined can do it."

"I don't know how long it would take someone to get the parts and assemble explosives like the ones used here," Cassie said. "If it can be done quickly, then I suppose it could be in response to one of the conversations we had today. Maybe we made somebody nervous." Cassie quickly listed the names of the people she and Leon had talked to throughout the day, adding a summary with each name to explain who they were and why she'd wanted to talk to them.

"Cassie!" Daisy Silverdeer, bounty hunter and Rock Solid's newest hire, hurried across the street. She wrapped her arms around Cassie and hugged her.

Daisy's husband, Martin, was close behind. Harry was also with them.

After multiple reassurances by Leon and Cassie that they were fine, Cassie quickly filled in their coworkers on the information they'd just given the detective.

Bergman asked the newly arriving bounty hunters if they had any idea who might have launched the attack. No one had a suggestion to offer.

"I know you don't work for me," Bergman said, his glance taking in everyone in the small group before finally settling on Cassie. "But if you decide to continue questioning people, please keep me in the loop. I'd like to know who you talk to, what they tell you, and if they behave suspiciously or not. My department is going to be working our own investigation, but as always, you might get info we don't get."

"Of course," Cassie said. She glanced toward the

building and then back at the sergeant. "I'll try to un-cover helpful information again as soon as I can. But first things first. I'll need to secure my office once the firefighters are finished." She sighed heavily. "I want to go in and have a look as soon as they say it's safe. Check for anything salvageable. And then I'll need to head to the ranch to grab some plywood so I can return to board up the broken windows."

"Go home," Harry said to her. "You can walk through the office and look for anything you want to save to-morrow. Meanwhile, Daisy and Martin and I can board things up."

"Yeah, let us take care of it," Martin added.

Cassie stole another glance at her burned-out office before turning back to Martin. "I'm not quite ready to go yet."

"Ready or not, you need to leave," Bergman said. *"Now."*

When Cassie turned to face him, he softened his ex-pression slightly. "My concern is that the person or per-sons who want you dead might be out here, watching and waiting for a chance to take a shot at you."

The cop's warning got Leon's attention. "Come on." He reached out to Cassie until she finally took his hand. "Let me take you home."

"All right," she said. "But we aren't giving up until we find whoever is behind all of this."

"That's right," Leon agreed. And then he sent up a silent prayer. *Please Lord, help us find them before they attack Cassie again.*

EIGHT

"We'll go riding again soon, I promise." Cassie reached up to scratch the cheek of her chestnut mare, Taffy, while gazing into the gentle horse's dark brown eyes. She'd turned the animal out in the small corral closest to the house so she could see her and talk to her while she did some chores. Given the events of the last few days, Cassie hadn't been out riding on the North Star Ranch property as much as usual. Poor Taffy had gotten lonesome, nickering at Cassie to beckon her whenever she saw her. The horse wanted Cassie's attention and today Cassie hadn't been able to refuse.

It was Sunday afternoon and the sky was a brilliant blue with a few white puffy clouds drifting slowly about. Cassie had been to church services in the morning after her pastor assured her that he did not want her to stay away despite the danger stalking her. Even after the explosions and gunfire at her office last night. In the end, arrangements were made for Martin and Harry to sit in their trucks and keep an eye on things outside the little country church while they listened to the livestreamed service. Meanwhile, everyone else would go inside.

The morning's sermon had been a strengthening respite in the midst of troubling times not just for Cassie, but for her dad and her friends, as well. The bounty hunters who worked for her were her friends and not simply employees. They'd made that clear repeatedly by their actions over the years. The same was true of Sherry and Jay, who had likewise been welcomed into the orbit of the Wheeler family.

...nor do we know what to do, but our eyes are upon You.

The topic for today's sermon was from the old testament. Sometimes, when life seemed to come at Cassie especially hard, she found comfort in the stories of people who'd had to face much more difficult circumstances than she had. And when she couldn't solve a troubling situation, and was beginning to feel hopeless, it gave her strength to be reminded that sometimes she didn't have to know what do to. She just needed to focus her thoughts on trusting the One who did know.

"Do you want to start working in the stables?" Leon asked, walking up beside Cassie at the corral rail. He reached out to scratch Taffy on the side of her toffee-colored neck, and she chuffed softly.

After church, everyone had gone back to the ranch for barbecued chicken and German potato salad. Following the meal, Harry and his wife, Ramona, had left to visit Ramona's parents for the afternoon. They'd been reluctant to leave, and it had taken a ridiculous amount of reassurance from Cassie to convince them that everyone would be fine without them and they should just go.

Martin and Daisy had stayed to ride the distant fence lines of the ranch with Adam and Jay. It was an extra bit of precaution as they checked to make sure that no one had cut a section of fence to give themselves easy access to the property. They'd also look for other signs, like tire tracks or footprints, that could indicate the bad guys were lining things up to launch an attack on the ranch house. Presumably when they thought Cassie was inside it.

Until very recently, she would have thought that idea absurd. But she would have also thought the idea of someone throwing explosive devices into her office—which wasn't that far from the police station—ridiculous.

Now she had to believe that anything was possible.

"Let's muck out the stalls first and then take care of food and fresh water," Cassie said. "We can check on the outdoor lights and security cameras after that." While all of the ranch's cameras appeared operational when she'd checked their feeds on her laptop, she wanted to make certain they had not been physically tampered with or prepped so that someone could disrupt them at a future time.

She did a lot of reading and research for her job. It was a frightening reality that sophisticated criminals planned ahead, conducted surveillance and sometimes used signal jamming or eavesdropping devices.

Leon turned and headed for the stables. Cassie trailed behind him, but not by much. It felt like every joint in her body was sore, however she was determined not to let the pain bring her to a halt.

She stepped into the stables where most of the stalls were empty at the moment. Earlier, they'd turned the horses out into the larger corral or the nearby pasture to get some sun and fresh air. Leon grabbed a rake and shovel and started mucking out one of the stalls. Cassie couldn't help feeling a tug at her heart, despite the less-than-romantic setting.

Leon was a man who took care of things. He took care of people. He took care of animals. He did it all so automatically, and without the need for acknowledgment, that it could be easy to take him for granted. And for an anxious moment or two, Cassie wondered if *she* had done that. Taken his loyalty for granted. And his big heart. That sometimes went unnoticed because he didn't exactly look like a sweet guy.

Right here, right now, she could literally be in the crosshairs of the scope on a rifle someone had pointed at her, sighting her through one of the open doors. There wasn't a whole lot she could do about that until she—or the police—figured out who kept coming after her and then finally put a stop to it. How many people would stay as close by her side through something like this as Leon had?

She grabbed a rake and shovel and set to work cleaning a stall, stealing another glance at the big bounty hunter when they were both in the main aisle getting fresh hay to put down. He worked fast and his movements were fluid and easy. He also kept an eye on what was going on around him. He was vigilant by nature. She knew that from all the time she'd spent working with him. But he was especially vigilant today. Understandably. Last night had been a terrifyingly close call.

He turned in her direction. Their eyes met and their gazes held. For the span of several heartbeats, they were both frozen, looking at one another. Leon's expression was unguarded, which was unusual for him. His eyes were an open window into the worry and concern he was feeling. And also held a tender regard for Cassie that took her by surprise.

She felt her breath catch, followed by a fluttering sensation of attraction in the center of her chest that she absolutely did not want. Not with an employee. Not with a male friend. Not with any man at all. Not now, or anytime soon. Not while the murder of her husband was still unsolved and she felt trapped in a state of emotional limbo.

These were not normal times, she reminded herself. The search for the people determined to kill her had reached a point of maximum intensity. Everybody was tired and they needed to lean on one another.

Even big, tough, Leon got tired sometimes. He needed someone to lean on. And Cassie was there.

That's what this unsettling, fluttering feeling was. It was simply an emotional moment after a grinding stretch of days spent just trying to stay alive. The wisp of deeper connection between the two of them that existed in this moment would vanish like haze as soon as one of them said something or looked away. It *had* to. Because he was her friend. Her rock. She wouldn't do anything to change the relationship they already had. She cherished it.

The man *worked for her*, she admonished herself in what was becoming a constant mental reminder. And she had her own personal set of guidelines when it came to crossing the line in that kind of situation.

Leon sighed heavily, the expression in his eyes settling into sorrow. He was the first to look away.

He got back to work. Sunlight shone on him through an open exterior door. Dust motes and bits of straw swirled around him and reflected the light as he leaned in and put his considerable muscles into what he was doing. As he basically put his *heart* into what he was doing.

She was using him. Cassie knew that now, because she realized he was holding on to the hope of a closer relationship between the two of them that was just not going to happen. She was taking advantage of his loyalty. Acknowledging that fact made her feel sick. And bitterly disappointed in herself.

She needed to make some changes. Immediately. And make sure she was no longer sending out signals she didn't intend to send. Signals that hinted he had a reason to hope they had a romantic future together, someday.

Cassie got back to work, determined not to let the current crisis she was in—trying to stay alive while following up on the first lead she'd had on Jake's murder in years—undermine her friendship with Leon.

"I can't figure out why anybody connected to Jake's murder would want *me* dead," Cassie said after they'd finished with the stalls. She'd been ruminating on the question the whole time she'd been mucking and then laying down fresh straw. It was something she'd considered before, but hadn't had time to think about. "It's not like getting rid of me would stop the police investigation."

"I've wondered about that, too," Leon said. "But I haven't come up with any good theories."

Things had gone back to feeling normal between the two of them, after an hour of hard, physical work, and Cassie was grateful for that. "I understand why Seth talking too much while he was drunk in a jail cell could make the people responsible for Jake's murder nervous.

But why would that make people who've already gotten away with murder want to stick their necks out now and come after me? Why not continue to lie low? Or get out of town—or the county—if you're that worried about being caught?"

Leon shrugged. "I don't know."

They put fresh water in each of the stalls, but Cassie didn't want to bring the horses back in yet. She wanted to let them enjoy a little more of the fresh air and sunshine. She stepped toward one of the open doors to feel the sun on her face and enjoy the beautiful surroundings.

"Standing right there, in the light and framed by the doorway, not moving, makes you an easy target," Leon said. "And from here, I can't see if there's anybody out there watching you. So maybe you want to stand somewhere else."

Right. A nervous tremor passed through her and she stepped back into the shaded interior of the stables, thinking about how she'd never felt unsafe here at the ranch before.

Duke and Tinker, both of whom liked to hang around the stables, lazily walked over to her and she gave each of the dogs a head scratch. And then she filled the food and water dishes for the barn cats. She glanced up to see one of them, Henry, on a crossbeam overhead, supervising her work.

"Shall we move on to checking the lights and security cameras?" Leon asked.

"Sure."

They began their walk around the buildings on the property to make a quick visual inspection of the equipment. Cassie forced herself to keep farther away from

Leon than she normally would when they walked together. No time like the present to reset the boundary lines of their relationship. Make it clear that they were coworkers and friends. But that was all. She simply couldn't offer him anything more. Even if she wanted to.

"Have you had time to think about the people we talked to yesterday?" Leon asked as they walked. "I realize there's been a lot going on, but right now, while it's quiet, if you consider each of them, does anybody seem suspicious to you? Or maybe even familiar, now that you think about it? Like they could have been one of the kidnappers who grabbed you? Or maybe one of the shooters in the forest? I'm inclined to think it was the same two men both times, but I never saw the kidnappers, so I don't know. And Bergman makes a good point when he says we shouldn't jump to conclusions."

"Nobody seemed familiar. No one told us anything that leads me any closer to knowing who Jake's killer was. Or *killers* were. Whichever it is." Cassie shook her head. "In my mind, I still have the same list of potential suspects. Including the drug supplier, Stefan Kasparov. He could very well have known the drug task force was watching him but didn't let on to anybody. He could have had one of his people kill Jake. Or, more recently, sent some of his people to kill me."

"Bombing a bail bonds office does sound like the kind of splashy, signal-sending thing an ambitious drug supplier would do," Leon said. "What about Rogan and Lutz?"

"I thought Bryan Rogan and his buddies might be behind the initial attack because they wanted to keep me from testifying against him. But after I gave the testimony, why continue the attacks? I have to consider the possibility. But why go to such extremes to carry out some kind of grudge?"

"So you don't think holding a grudge is good enough motivation for all of this?" Leon asked. "Does that mean you don't suspect Jerry Lutz anymore?"

Cassie thought for a few moments before shaking her head. "I wouldn't take Lutz off the suspect list just yet. His grudge was different. Very personal and all-consuming. He was convinced that Jake ruined his marriage and his life when he arrested him. That's a strong motivation. But it still leaves a whole lot of questions unanswered."

As they walked, the dogs stayed close by, supervising their work. Tinker and Duke weren't exactly guard dogs, but they would bark if someone came around the house. Unless they'd just eaten a big bowl of broth-soaked kibble and were sacked out on their fleece-lined dog beds fast asleep. In which case a band of marauders could break in to ransack the place and they wouldn't stir. Spoiled mutts.

In the distance, Adam, Jay, Martin and Daisy broke through the tree line, heading for the stables then slowing to cool their horses. Cassie lifted her arm in a wave and they waved back. Then she checked her phone. There were no messages from any of them, so she figured no one had seen anything out of the ordinary.

"I can check the security gate at the end of the drive if you want to go talk to them," Leon said.

"No, I'll go with you."

It wasn't like he was offering to make some great sacrifice, going to the end of the long unpaved drive. But she had to stop letting him do so many things for her. She couldn't let things continue to feel so personal between them. She *wouldn't* do that. She thought too much of him to allow that to continue.

Normally, Leon was so easy to talk to. And that made it especially frustrating that she couldn't talk to him about *this*. This weird *whatever* between the two of them. Because maybe her concerns were just her ego talking. Maybe he wasn't doing anything for her that he wouldn't do for anyone else. Maybe she just needed to get over herself.

"Let's take my truck," he said. "Just to be safe."

"Right." Walking around the cluster of buildings well inside the property was one thing. Walking out to the road where anyone could easily get close and take a shot at her, or at both of them, was something different, and riskier.

They drove to the gate, where Cassie hopped out to quickly check the video camera, data relay equipment and power source connections.

Leon stood nearby, head on a swivel, his gaze sweeping the surroundings.

"So now I think Kasparov is our best suspect," Leon said while Cassie worked. "Because you're right, he could have known that Jake was part of a law enforcement task force looking to bring down drug suppliers. And killed him for that reason. He would have people he could order to kill you now."

"Yeah, but that still circles back to the question of why try so hard to kill me?" Cassie used the hem of her shirt to clean off the video camera lens.

Leon tilted his head. A sign, Cassie knew, that he was seriously pondering something. "If you want to establish a powerful criminal enterprise, it's important that people fear you. Maybe it has something to do with that. He could be protecting his turf and his image. Maybe there's some power struggle going on and he thinks killing you would send a signal to someone he's battling right now. That old threat to kill somebody and their family, too, is still a powerful deterrent."

"Well, that's chilling," Cassie said, thinking not just of herself but also of the fact that that kind of behavior actually existed in the world. It seemed like her career as a bail bondswoman and bounty hunter should keep her from getting shocked by criminal activities, but it didn't.

"The investigation into Stefan Kasparov is something we're going to have to leave up to Sergeant Bergman," Cassie said. "Talking to Travis at the bodega and getting baseline information on Kasparov is about as far as we can go. Anything more could disrupt an ongoing police investigation." Not to mention put her whole family and all of her employees in serious danger. If she ultimately decided there was something further in the realm of Kasparov's drug empire that she needed to look into, she would do it on her own. She would not drag anyone else along with her.

With her inspection of the gate completed, they got into the truck and headed up to the house where she'd check with her dad just to make certain he and the other riders hadn't seen anything unusual. As the truck rolled along, Cassie glanced in the side mirror at the gate behind them. She felt a little bit better now that she and Leon and the others had checked the security of the ranch and its perimeter. But she didn't think their effort would keep them safe. At best, it would likely just slow the inevitable arrival of another attack.

* * *

Monday morning, Leon stood beside Cassie in the parking lot behind Rock Solid Bail Bonds. They'd been inside earlier because Cassie had wanted to inspect the damage. It had been pretty extensive. Leon was glad to be out of the office, away from the lingering, petroleum-like scent of smoke, and back in the fresh air. The door, with the damage from the shooting patched over, was propped open in an attempt to clear things out.

Sergeant Bergman, who'd just arrived, stood facing the two of them. Cassie had called him last night for an update on whatever information he had, and his response had been a text telling her to meet with him this morning.

"We've got some basic information about the incendiary devices thrown in here," Bergman said after greeting Leon and Cassie. "They were obviously effective, and simple to make. The various parts are easy to find. The Feds will check to see if any element of the bombing matches the signature of any known arsonist in the area, or if there's any profiling information they can give us. But that will take time."

"Of course," Cassie said.

Leon admired how strong she'd remained through this whole horrible string of events. But he was also worried that the emotional trauma and physical punishment were getting to her. She seemed distant and more aloof than usual both last night and this morning.

"We're taking a close look at everyone you talked to Saturday," Bergman continued. "We'll check to see if any of them has a connection to a known arsonist or anyone with a suspected bomb-making history."

"Stefan Kasparov seems a good possibility for that," Leon said. "We didn't talk to him. But we did talk to Travis Jefferson *about* him."

"Kasparov and his people have a track record of violence," Bergman said. "I haven't heard of them being connected to anything like this fire-bombing, but there's a first time for everything."

"What's the possibility that Jake was investigating something you didn't know about when he was murdered?" Cassie asked. "Maybe something that was kept secret and confidential for some reason."

"I have wondered that myself," Bergman said.

"And?"

He slightly quirked an eyebrow. "I don't have an answer for you right now. My understanding is that the agencies involved in the investigation of his murder, including the Stone River Police Department, were given all pertinent information related to the task force he was working with. It would be pretty bad for law enforcement employee morale if the investigation into a cop's murder was impeded for the sake of a criminal investigation. Especially if information needed to solve the murder was still being kept hidden five years down the road." He sighed. "I don't think it's likely anything has been held back. But I do want to be thorough, so I'm having someone audit the information we have to see if there appears to be anything missing."

"Thank you," Cassie said. "What about the possible address I texted you for Seth Tatum? Is that correct?"

She'd told Leon that she didn't want to put Bergman on the spot by asking for information he may not be allowed to share, but asking him to confirm information after she'd uncovered it on her own seemed reasonable. Even if Seth no longer lived in Saddleback, it could be worth the trip over there to talk to people who knew him.

"Seth moved over to Montana shortly after he graduated from high school. The address you have for him is the most recent address we have. But there still hasn't been any sighting of him."

"Which makes this a perfect time for us to do what we do best," Leon said, hoping to cheer up Cassie. "We want to go talk to his neighbors, his coworkers and anybody else who won't talk to the cops but who will talk to us."

"Yeah, I figured that's what you'd say." Bergman turned to Cassie. "I understand how important this investigation is to you. But you've already done an excellent job at heating up your husband's cold case. Don't you need to stay here and fix up your office? Keep your business running by being around to meet with new clients? Maybe even rest up a little after all you've been through?"

"My dad will be meeting the insurance adjuster here later this morning," Cassie told him. "The repairs are his project for now. Harry is working with our part-time bounty hunter, Carlos Flanagan, to get a handle on the daily business issues."

"I hope that means your other two bounty hunters are going with you to look for Seth."

Cassie gestured toward the truck that had just turned into the parking lot with Daisy and Martin inside. "I told them to be here by nine and to plan for a day trip to Montana."

Bergman's phone rang. He glanced at the screen. "Watch your backs," he said to Cassie and Leon before putting the phone to his ear and then turning and walking to his unmarked police car.

Martin and Daisy got out of their truck and walked up carrying a shopping bag. "We brought snacks and bottled water," Daisy called out. "This one's for you." She handed over the bag. They'd decided to take two separate vehicles for the trip to Montana.

"You know, none of you needs to do this." Cassie looked at the three bounty hunters surrounding her. "It's not your job. It's not a requirement to stay employed with me. And the situation is getting very dangerous. Besides, Harry and Carlos might need some help. Any one of you would be doing me a favor if you stayed behind and helped them."

When she shifted her gaze to make eye contact with Leon, he felt a flare of emotion somewhere between insult and anger. How could she possibly think he'd want to stay behind and let her go to Montana without him?

Their gazes stayed locked for several long seconds, until Cassie finally dropped hers and looked away. And Leon had the disquieting feeling that she was holding something back from him.

Daisy, who'd been standing beside Cassie, bumped her lightly with her shoulder. "Don't be ridiculous. We're all going. Everybody loves a road trip. So quit stalling, lock the back door to your office, and let's roll."

Cassie's eyes got very shiny. Like she was about to start crying. And Leon felt a knot form in the center of his chest.

He was wary of this outing. They would be driving through long stretches of forested wilderness on the trip over the mountain pass from Idaho into Montana. It was perfect ambush country.

Meanwhile, Cassie was losing her edge. He could see it. On a personal level he felt bad for her and what she was going through. Beyond that, he was worried that fatigue and emotional exhaustion might make her see or hear something—like a footfall or a twig snapping— just a second too late. And that could be the end for her.

NINE

Saddleback, Montana, was located ten miles east of the college town of Jameson. It was a community of maybe five thousand people spread across forested foothills. Cassie was excited at the prospect of finding Seth and finally getting a lead on who murdered her husband. But at the same time, she tried not to let herself get her hopes up too much.

Leon turned down a shady street lined with big, leafy trees about six blocks from what passed for the downtown section of Saddleback. The houses here were small, with detached garages, and looked like they'd been built at least fifty years ago. Several had chain-link fences surrounding their front yards.

Roughly midway down the block they found the house with the number they were looking for. The first thing Cassie noticed was the overgrown lawn. As Leon pulled up to the curb, she saw the overstuffed mailbox beside the front door.

"It could be that Seth is hiding inside and just trying to make it look like he hasn't been home in a while," Leon said, correctly anticipating Cassie's thoughts. She was already fighting the deflating sensation that this trip would end up all for nothing.

"We'll start with the assumption he could be in there," Cassie said, "and work from there."

Martin and Daisy had already pulled up behind them alongside the curb. Normally, for the sake of efficiency, they would have worked as two separate teams on two separate tasks. One team at the house and another at Seth's last known place of employment. But right now the priority was safety—for everyone, not just Cassie— and that meant they would stick together.

They got out of their trucks and met up on the sidewalk. "Leon and I will knock on the front door," Cassie said, anxious to move quickly in case Seth actually was inside. She didn't want to give him time to see her or to figure out who she was or why this small group of people might be there. She also didn't want to linger where they might be spotted by a neighbor who might call Seth—wherever he was—to tell him what was going on right now in front of his house.

"Martin, you stay out here on the sidewalk so you're ready to go after Seth if he sprints from the garage or a neighbor's house or a parked car or somewhere else," she continued. "Daisy, I want you by the gate to the backyard. If you hear anything, it could be him trying to hop his back fence and get away. Let us know and we'll chase after him."

They all had radios and did a quick check to make sure they were working properly. Cassie had a brief flashback to her recent abduction and forced herself to mentally set it aside. She had plenty of experience with bypassing emotions and dealing with them later. Maybe that wasn't the healthiest thing to do, but in her line of work—and with her life experience—she had found it necessary.

"Seth is officially in violation of his bond, right?" Daisy said. "So we can legally chase him and arrest him if he tries to run?"

"Absolutely," Cassie answered. "His parents secured the bond for his driving under the influence charge through an agency in Boise, where they live. They moved down there from Stone River about three years ago. I contacted the bondsman there after I was able to confirm Seth's identity. Since he was a no-show for his court date, his bond is vacated. The bondsman will pay us a recovery fee if we catch him, so at the least, we'll earn the cost for the trip here plus the day's wages for everybody." No one had asked, but Cassie wanted to make sure they knew they'd be paid. She was not going to let them do this for free as a favor to her.

"All right," she said, "let's get to work."

Martin stayed where he was while Daisy headed for the gate at the side of the residence.

Cassie and Leon headed up the cement walkway from the sidewalk to the front steps, keeping an eye on the windows and the glass pane in the door for a moving shadow, fluttering curtains or any other sign that someone was inside.

Cassie knocked politely. If she didn't sound threatening, and Seth was in there, he might be more likely to answer the door. If he didn't answer, she'd get a little more insistent. Pound a little louder. It could be that he was someone more likely to respond if he was stressed or afraid.

Leon stayed a few feet behind her, near the bottom

of the steps, where he had a wider view of the door and windows.

There was no answer, so she tried knocking again. Eventually, Cassie ended up pounding on the door and calling out Seth's name. But there was no response. She didn't hear any sounds from inside the house, and the only footprints in the light layer of dust on the doorstep were her own.

She turned to Leon and shook her head, struggling to keep the disappointment out of her voice. "I don't think he's here."

Of course he wasn't. What were the odds that he would be? But she'd let herself hope because she'd *needed* to hope. Told herself that he'd hidden from the local cops when they'd come by to check things out at Sergeant Bergman's request, but that he might show himself to a civilian.

"Does his mail look like it's been sitting there for a while?" Leon asked, gesturing at the overstuffed box.

Cassie glanced at the edges of envelopes and a couple of thin catalogs that were in plain view. "None of it appears especially weathered," she said. "But a couple of pieces look a little dusty, like maybe they've been sitting in the mailbox for a few days. Looks like he hasn't collected his mail for about a week."

She'd turned and headed down the steps when a man came barreling toward them from the house next door. He called out, "Hey you! What are you people doing?"

"Hi. We're looking for Seth," Cassie said smoothly. "Do you know where he is?"

"Well, he isn't inside his mailbox." The man, skinny and maybe in his mid-fifties, shoved his hands onto his hips and jutted out his chin. "I saw you looking at it. This is private property, you know."

Cassie glanced at the house next door to Seth's, noting the side window with its open shades and coffee mug on the windowsill. If this guy was a nosy neighbor, he could turn out to be helpful. But she'd need him to calm down first.

"Do you know Seth?" she asked.

"I'm his neighbor so, yeah, obviously." The guy wagged his head as though he'd made a brilliant point.

"When is the last time you saw him?"

"What's it to ya?"

Cassie took a calming breath, reminding herself that this man could simply be a good citizen looking out for his neighbor. "My name is Cassie," she said. "And I just want to ask him a few questions."

The neighbor cocked an eyebrow. "Why don't you just use a phone like everybody else?"

"I've tried, but I don't get an answer. Maybe it's broken or he lost it." Bergman had not authorized her to share the fact that, according to police, the known phone for Seth had vanished off the grid. No signal. No response to a ping. No GPS location. Nothing.

"Maybe he just doesn't want to talk to you," the neighbor countered.

Cassie sighed. She was going to have to take a chance. "Seth may have come across some trouble," she said. "He's a good guy. I just want to help him out."

If it turned out to be common knowledge that Seth *wasn't* a good guy, this conversation would likely come to an abrupt end.

The neighbor—who hadn't offered his name, and Cassie wasn't inclined to press him for it—relaxed his stance a little. Likewise, his fixed glare softened and he looked away for a moment before turning back to Cassie. "I don't know if you really believe what you just said." He eyed her shrewdly. "But, like I told the cops when they came around, Seth's a nice guy and a considerate neighbor. Keeps to himself, but there's nothing wrong with that. Doesn't mean he's a serial killer or something."

Cassie kept silent. Mentioning that she wanted to talk to him regarding the unsolved murder of her husband wouldn't likely be helpful. "Do you know where he is right now?" she asked softly and carefully, not wanting to blow an opportunity to find him if one hung in the balance.

"I don't."

"When and where is the last time you saw him?" Cassie held her breath for a few seconds, waiting to see if the man would answer her question or tell her to go away. It was situations like these, where she had to quickly get a read on someone and possibly get them to calm down, that her experience really helped. Chasing after fugitives and wrestling them to the ground if necessary was something anyone who was fit and trained could do. But reading people and situations? That was often trickier.

The neighbor bit down on his lip and considered her question. "The last time I saw Seth was maybe ten days ago? Something like that. He was heading to Stone River in Idaho. It was for a wedding or maybe a big birthday party. He seemed kind of excited and nervous at the same time. I was happy for him. The guy just works and stays inside that house alone most of the time."

Maybe, Cassie thought. *Or maybe Seth just wants things to appear that way.*

"It was kind of odd," the neighbor added. "He left, came back maybe three days later, and then after that he vanished. Left his car behind in the garage. You can see it through the window."

"Do you have any idea where he might have gone the second time?" Cassie pressed, figuring the nosy neighbor might have gotten at least a scrap of information out of Seth.

The neighbor shook his head. "It was at night when he came back from that initial trip. After dark. I was already in my pajamas. I didn't go outside to talk to him."

"Thank you for your help." Cassie gestured at Leon to come closer. "We'd like to leave one of our business cards with you in case you think of something later or maybe you see or hear from Seth."

Leon reached into his back pocket for his wallet to retrieve a business card. Cassie had left all of hers in her purse, which was locked in the truck at the moment.

Leon held out the card and the neighbor reached for it.

"There's a cash award for additional information," Cassie added.

The man looked at the card and went back to squinting at her. "You're from a bail bond company? What exactly is going on?"

She forced a lighthearted smile on her face. "I'd really prefer to talk to him about that. And remember, we pay for information."

She and Leon offered a few polite parting words then turned and walked over to meet Daisy and Martin by the trucks.

"What did you learn?" Daisy asked.

"Not much," Cassie responded.

"Did you check the trash bins while we talked to him?" Leon asked Martin.

The younger bounty hunter glanced at the two dark green bins in the driveway near the garage door and nodded. "Yep. They're completely empty. Nothing to indicate that anyone is actually inhabiting the house and generating garbage. There's a little bit of dust and pine straw on the lids and surrounding ground. Doesn't look like they've been moved in a while. I also took a quick peek in the window on the side of the garage. There's a car parked in there that's the same make, model and color as the one that we know is registered to Seth."

"He's probably gotten another vehicle to use," Cassie said. "Something that's not registered to him." She took a deep breath and let it out.

"Okay, let's check the neighbors on the other side of Seth's house and across the street. Then let's get out of here," she continued as a car drove by and the occupants looked over at the bounty hunters. "I don't want us to draw a lot of attention to ourselves."

Cassie and Leon headed across the street, where the woman who answered the door listened impatiently to Cassie's quick introduction and request for information about Seth. The woman made it clear she wasn't interested in talking to them and closed the door in their faces. Cassie asked for another business card from Leon, tucked it between the closed door and doorframe, and then called out, "We pay for information. I'll leave our contact number out here."

They walked back to their trucks, where Daisy met

them, shaking her head. "Nobody was home next door. We left a card. Wrote a short note on the back."

"Did the note mention we'd pay for information?"

"Of course."

Cassie glanced around, wondering if Seth was somewhere nearby, watching them. He could have been hiding in the house with the nosy next-door neighbor. She hadn't gotten what she'd come for, namely, a face-to-face conversation with Seth. But she did feel like she'd taken hold of the end of a thread that might eventually unravel something. Maybe someone would call to talk to her later.

"One goal down, one to go." She clapped her hands together. "Let's head to the center of town and check out Seth's workplace." It wasn't too far-fetched to think he might need money badly enough that he'd kept his job even if he'd stopped going home at night.

"Seth *was* employed here. But he took a couple days off for what was supposed to be a short trip over to Idaho and he never came back. Ricky, the manager, says that because he never even bothered to call in, Seth's been fired."

Leon nodded at the friendly young guy working behind the counter near the loading dock at Lawson's Discount Furniture. He had the name Buzz embroidered on his work shirt.

Cassie was wandering around in the showroom on the other side of the large building, with Daisy and Martin following along to discreetly keep an eye on her and their surroundings. Oftentimes several bounty hunters walking into an establishment together and looking too intimidating caused people to clam up. So they'd split up, with Leon in the warehouse area and Cassie up front looking to talk to a salesperson or the manager.

"Do you know Seth very well?" Leon asked just before a loud truck drove by on the street outside. The warehouse's roll-up dock doors had been tied open to let the warm breeze stir the air. The dimness inside the structure made the sunny world outside look glaringly bright.

"Seth and I didn't hang out together much, if that's what you're asking," Buzz said after the rumble of the passing truck died down. "Are you a cop or something?"

Leon shook his head. "No. I just want to ask him some questions."

"Why do people keep showing up here looking for him?"

"You mean like cops?"

"Cops." Buzz nodded. "And a couple of other guys who said they weren't cops and didn't seem like cops. And now you."

Leon's heart sped up. "The guys who didn't seem like cops. Did they tell you their names?"

"No."

"Can you tell me what they looked like?"

"I don't remember. They were just regular-looking guys. We were really busy when they came by and they weren't here for long. Is Seth in trouble?"

"Would you be surprised if he were?" Sometimes indirect questions elicited more information.

Buzz shrugged his shoulders. "Something's got to be going on when a guy suddenly stops showing up at work and then a parade of people come around asking questions about him." He gave Leon an appraising look. "Does Seth owe you money? Is that why you're here?"

This wasn't the first time someone had assumed Leon

was a kneecap breaker. "He doesn't owe me any money," Leon said, trying to seem nonthreatening. Maybe this guy was actually a close friend of Seth's and knew where he was hiding. "I just want to help him out. And anyone who gives me information could stay anonymous."

Buzz gave him a doubtful look.

"Can you tell me where Seth likes to spend his time when he's not at home or at work?"

Considering how small the town was, it was likely Buzz had seen him around even if they weren't buddies.

"I don't know where he likes to hang out," Buzz said as a Lawson's Discount Furniture truck backed up to one of the loading bays. "Excuse me." He stepped out from behind the work counter and headed toward a pallet jack stationed by one of the freight doors.

Leon watched for a few minutes as Buzz and the truck driver loaded a sofa and a couple of easy chairs onto the truck. After the truck pulled away from the dock and turned onto the street, Buzz briefly glanced at Leon then walked away in the opposite direction. Their conversation was obviously over.

Leon crossed the cement floor to the entrance into the carpeted showroom, anxious to tell Cassie about the other men who'd been here inquiring about Seth. He saw her talking to a salesman. Martin and Daisy were standing in front of a couch just a few feet away, holding hands. To a casual observer it might appear that they were focused on the furniture. But Leon could see that they were keeping an eye on the showroom and on Cassie.

The salesman seemed quite focused on Cassie, smiling and leaning close to her as he talked. Maybe he was just being friendly so he could make a sale. But it was also possible he was flirting.

Though he wasn't thrilled to witness it, Leon couldn't blame the guy. Cassie was the most attractive woman he knew.

She was also someone he counted among his friends. Although last night and today he'd felt an increasing distance between them. Maybe it was because she was scared. Or maybe it was because she was physically exhausted. She'd been through a lot.

Whatever was happening was not about *him*, he reminded himself. And how he felt about it all didn't matter. Right now, everything was about helping Cassie hold herself together while pursuing her husband's killer. And trying to make sure they all stayed alive.

Cassie took a step back from the salesman, saying, "Thank you. Any information you could pass along would be very helpful." She had her purse with her and reached in for a business card.

Leon started heading in her direction so he'd be beside her when she stepped out the door to the parking lot.

"And it would be treated confidentially, of course," Cassie continued as she handed the card to the salesman. A little more quietly, she added, "We do pay for information."

As Cassie headed for the door, Leon glanced over at Daisy and Martin, and the three of them followed her out to the parking lot. When they caught up to her, Leon told them that someone other than police had showed up at the furniture store looking for Seth.

They spent the rest of the afternoon stopping by grocery stores, convenience stores, gas stations and fast-food restaurants showing people Seth's photo and asking if they knew him or had recently seen him. Despite their best intentions, fugitives often tended to fall back into old habits despite their intention to stay hidden.

As expected in a fairly small community, they'd come across several people who'd recognized Seth's picture. But none had had any idea where he was. At least, not that they'd admit to.

At the end of the day, after subsisting on protein bars and energy drinks, Cassie sprang for a nice dinner at a steakhouse recommended by Daisy in nearby Jameson. With a hearty meal under their belts, they climbed into their trucks and headed back to Stone River.

"It looks like Seth really did leave town," Cassie said to Leon as they crested a hill west of town. "I need to figure out where I want to look for him next."

She'd checked her email when she'd first gotten into the truck after dinner and seen lots of messages from her dad about the insurance adjuster and the process for getting the office rebuilt. All tedious stuff she really didn't want to deal with right now.

The truth was she took care of the business side of things at Rock Solid Bail Bonds because she had to. Her favorite aspect of it all was the actual chase for a fugitive. Especially when she had Leon around to back her up. She glanced over at his profile, tried not to admire it too much, and then shifted her attention to the side mirror where she saw the headlights of Martin's truck behind them.

"The first logical place to look for Seth would be at his parents' house in Boise," Leon said.

"Yeah, but if he's hiding because his life is in danger, or he thinks it is, his parents won't give him up."

"Maybe we can get across how sincere we are in our willingness to help and protect him."

They drove in forested darkness. There weren't many vehicles on the road. From here to the eastern edge of Stone River in Idaho, they would make a significant rise in elevation as they traveled through the mountain pass.

Bang! Bang! Bang!

Bullets tore through the windshield of Leon's truck.

"Get down!" Leon hollered.

Behind them, Martin blared his horn to let them know he saw what had just happened.

Cassie ducked, but only long enough to grab her gun, roll down her window and ready herself to fire a few rounds. There was no way she would hide and put Leon in danger on his own.

"Drive faster!" she yelled. "We've got to get through the pass or we're done for!" She looked at the surrounding ridges. "Shooter's up ahead on the south side of the highway," she said, after seeing a short burst of illumination, probably from a flashlight.

Leon's phone rang and Cassie could see that it was Daisy calling. She touched the console screen to answer. "Are either of you hit?" Cassie demanded by way of a greeting.

"No," Daisy said. "Are you?"

"No." Cassie glanced over at Leon. In the glow from the dashboard lights, she could see blood on his face. Her breath caught in her throat. "Wait, Leon's been hit."

"It's nothing," he said, his voice tight with tension.

That was his standard reply no matter how badly he was hurt. It did not give Cassie any comfort.

"Martin's talking to the cops right now," Daisy said.

Cassie could hear her say to her husband, "Tell them to roll an ambulance, too."

"The jerk who shot at us is on top of the pass, on the south side," Cassie said, desperately wishing she could see into the surrounding darkness. "At least one of them is. There could be more. We can't stop or they'll pin us down and finish us off."

"Understood," Daisy said. "We're right behind you."

The headlights from Martin's truck drew closer to their back window.

Bang! Bang!

More gunshots. Cassie braced for another spray of broken glass, but then realized the shots sounded more muffled this time. And that the headlights from Martin's truck were suddenly extinguished.

"Daisy!" Cassie called out.

Through the speaker, she heard a jumble of sounds and Daisy's jostled voice calling out, "Our tire's been shot out."

"Stop!" Cassie yelled to Leon, reaching for his arm. "You've got to stop so we can help them."

"You said it yourself," he said grimly. "If we stop, we're dead. *You're* dead. They're after you, not Daisy and Martin. We need to get you away."

"No!" Cassie insisted. "Go back! You have to go back! I will not run away and leave them behind. I will *not*." She was so frantic, there were tears rolling down her cheeks. At any other time, she would have been mortified. Right now, she didn't even care.

Leon took his foot off the accelerator. He faced her, his expression stony.

"Please," she said.

Looking none too thrilled with her supplications,

he flipped a U-turn and headed back toward Martin's truck, which was off the side of the highway, partially hidden by an outcropping of rocks and surrounded by a few trees. Leon steered toward the truck and drove off the road until he was right beside it.

"It's us!" Cassie shouted into the phone, thinking Martin and Daisy might be unnerved at the sight of headlights coming directly at them.

"Copy," Daisy replied, sounding shaky.

Leon and Cassie quickly found Martin and Daisy crouched on the forest floor, using the segments of rock and their truck as a barricade. They quickly ducked down alongside them.

Bang! Bang!

More gunshots sounded, bullets ricocheting off the tops of the chunks of granite. Finally, the shooting stopped. Maybe the shooter had lost track of where they were hiding. Or maybe he knew exactly where they were and was moving closer to them. Maybe there was a second shooter even closer than they realized. Cassie's heart thundered in her chest as the four bounty hunters drew their weapons.

And then she saw a flash of blue light through the trees.

Martin still had an open line with the 9-1-1 dispatcher. "Do you see our officers?" she asked, her voice sounding tinny through his cell.

"Yes," Martin said.

"Thank You, Lord," Cassie whispered.

"Amen," Leon said quietly beside her.

Cassie turned to him and then reached out to place her fingers under his chin and gently turn his face toward her. On his cheek and forehead, she saw cuts and scratches from the spray of glass that had resulted from the bullets blasting through the truck's window.

She had seen him hurt worse, over the years. Much worse. Nevertheless, her heart felt like it had moved up into her throat. It was one thing to understand that her life was in danger. It was something altogether worse to realize that Leon could have been killed because he was protecting her.

He shifted his gaze to look directly into her eyes. The combination of tenderness and fierce determination she saw there nearly knocked the breath out of Cassie. She wondered if the expression in her eyes looked the same.

Before she realized what was happening, she did something completely out of character and pressed her lips against his uninjured cheek. And she lingered there, just for a moment, taking refuge in the warm feel of his skin and the mingling of their breaths.

Finally, she recovered her senses and leaned back. Where was her promise to herself to put some distance between them? What was the matter with her?

"Looks like we might live to see another day," she said shakily, trying her best to put a tone of detachment in her voice.

Leon cocked an eyebrow. "The day's not over yet."

TEN

Leon sat in the office at North Star Ranch with an empty coffee mug by his hand. It was shortly past eight on Tuesday morning and he'd nearly polished off an entire pot of coffee since he'd woken up around six.

The bounty hunters had spent a couple of hours with the local cops last night after the attack on the highway. Some of that time had been spent at the actual scene of the shooting. Some back at the Jameson police station explaining to the duty sergeant who they were, why they'd been in the area, and filling them in on the details of the previous attacks on Cassie's life.

Officers had searched the fire access road near the ridge where the shots fired at the bounty hunters had originated, but they hadn't found anyone up there. They planned to go back after sunrise to search for evidence that the shooter or shooters might have left behind.

Meanwhile, Leon's truck had been towed into Jameson to have the windshield repaired. Daisy, who had grown up in Jameson, had called a friend who'd promised to make Leon's truck repair his top priority.

The two-hour drive back to Stone River in Martin's truck, which had only required a tire change and the replacement of broken bulbs in the headlights to make it road worthy, had been fairly quiet. After they'd reached town, it was another twenty-minute ride out to the ranch. By the time Adam, Sherry and Jay had talked to each of the bounty hunters, and made certain every single one of them was okay, it was two in the morning. Martin and Daisy had wearily climbed back into Martin's truck and headed to their home in town.

The North Star household had turned in shortly after that. Leon had trudged into the spare room, dropped onto the bed while he was still fully clothed, and immediately fallen asleep. Only to have his eyelids pop open a mere four hours later, around six o'clock, as he jolted awake from a nightmare that had Cassie in a fiery crash on the highway where he couldn't rescue her in time.

He knew there would be no more sleep for him after that. Because while the events that had flickered through his mind while he was asleep were just a dream, the danger to Cassie was *real*. So he'd rolled out of bed, showered and dressed, and headed downstairs to drink coffee while mentally reviewing last night's events and checking the video security feeds.

Of course, Adam, Sherry and Jay had already been up, having coffee themselves along with their breakfast. This was a working ranch, after all. And Adam had already checked the security feeds. Still, Leon had wanted to take a fast-forwarded look at the recordings himself. Just to make sure there was no sign of anyone creeping around on the property. And since the others were up and keeping an eye on the ranch house, he decided to go outside to check the other buildings and make certain no one was hiding out there, waiting for a chance to shoot at Cassie again.

Tinker and Duke had accompanied him outside, both dogs crazy happy for attention and the adventure they seemed to think a walk with Leon offered.

Nothing appeared amiss at the outbuildings. The electric gate at the highway was securely closed and didn't appear to have been tampered with. All things he would be checking again soon. Because while life experience had taught him a long time ago that no single day could be taken for granted, last night's attack had vividly reminded him of that lesson.

He hadn't eaten breakfast because he hadn't had an appetite. His stomach was in knots and, rather than pick at a plate of scrambled eggs and sausage at the dining table while attempting to be sociable, he'd really wanted to get to work in the office. Where he could research the various people they'd contacted yesterday.

Tracking down details about people with the barest scrap of information to start with was often the focus of his day's work. He had the address of Seth's nosy neighbor. He had the address of the determined-not-to-help neighbor across the street. He had the name of Seth's employer, as well as the guy at the dock, Buzz. He'd gotten the name of the salesman from Cassie. He'd start searching public records to see what he could put together.

After the ambush on the mountain pass, Leon was even more determined to somehow tie the whole series of attacks together. Even if he didn't yet know what precise bits of information he was looking for. It was like putting together a puzzle without knowing ahead of time what the picture was going to look like.

Leon needed to organize a timeline of who Cassie had made contact with since Phil had told her about

Seth and she'd started asking questions as she'd tried to identify him. And he needed to figure out exactly who had known the bounty hunters would be traveling through the mountain pass at the time of night that they had. Was it someone they'd talked to or who had seen them while they were in Saddleback? Was it someone who had followed them from Stone River?

Had an accomplice called the shooter to let him know when they'd be heading toward the pass? Could someone have placed an electronic tracker on Leon's truck?

Points of information, names and faces and dates swirled around in his mind. It seemed like the disorganized puzzle pieces were too much to put together, particularly since they would go back to an unsolved murder from five years ago. But he would keep at it.

In the midst of sorting through the information he had, Leon closed his eyes and bowed his head in prayer, asking for strength and guidance and protection for Cassie and the entire Rock Solid Bail Bonds family. He'd just breathed a quiet "Amen" when he heard the soft sound of someone clearing their throat and opened his eyes to see Cassie standing in the doorway.

"Hey," she said softly. "I didn't mean to interrupt you. But I didn't want you to be startled when you opened your eyes and saw me standing here." She crossed her arms over her chest and leaned against the door frame. "With everything that's been happening, I think we're all on edge right now. Myself included."

She smiled self-consciously and Leon's heart softened. He thought of the kiss she'd given him last night. And then immediately tried *not* to, as his face warmed.

She was dressed in jeans and a light blue T-shirt. Her reddish hair was damp, and he could see the lines from where she'd just combed it. A familiar scent drifted from her direction. Lemongrass and ginger. He was fairly certain it came from her shampoo. And, like her, it was at once familiar and exotic.

Leon had spent so much time working with Cassie that he could usually anticipate her moves when they were about to capture a fugitive, and he could pretty accurately gauge her reaction to most situations. He spent a fair amount of time at the North Star Ranch even when he wasn't living here trying to protect her. He was friends with her dad.

And yet there were some of her thoughts that he had no clue about. He might not ever know. They probably weren't any of his business, anyway. But he did wonder what she planned for her future, since she'd mentioned it on their drive to the office on Saturday. What would make her happy? What did she envision? He wanted to know so that he could ready himself for the time when she met a man, fell in love again, and moved on with her life. Something he knew was inevitable. And he would celebrate with her when that happened, because he wanted her to be happy.

He found himself wondering how she saw *him*. Leon. Did she consider him as anything more than a solid friend and a familiar coworker, or was he simply one of her trusted bounty hunters? Did she see him as he was now? Or did she see him tarnished by his past?

He realized he'd let his gaze linger on her a little too long and quickly looked away.

Cassie cleared her throat. "I wanted to get in here, open up my laptop and do some research on the people we talked to yesterday."

She hadn't moved from her position in the doorway,

and it now registered with Leon that she had held that lingering, wordless gaze between the two of them for as long as he had before he'd looked away. What did that mean? If anything. Once again, she was familiar and unfathomable at the same time.

He *really* needed for this whole sprawling case to get wrapped up quickly so he could go back to staying in his own home every night. He was spending too much time around Cassie, and he was beginning to feel emotionally tangled up with her in a way that would never work out as he might hope.

"Great minds think alike," he said. Not an especially original quip, but it gave him an excuse to turn his eyes to his computer, roll his chair back slightly and gesture at the screen. "I've been putting together a spreadsheet of everyone we've made contact with."

She moved to him to have a look at his work.

"How are you feeling this morning?" he asked. "If I were you, I'd take today off and rest."

"Try that line with someone else," she said dryly. "I know you better than that."

She stood to his side, looking at the screen as he scrolled through to give her a quick look at what he'd done. "I haven't had time to dive into all the deep research yet," he said.

"While we're out in the field, we can get my dad started looking into some of this. He'd enjoy doing it. Email him what you have and copy me in."

Leon moved his empty mug to better reach the mouse.

"Is there coffee?" Cassie asked. "I could use some."

"You should eat something," Leon muttered as he

clicked a few times and sent the email. "You can't live on coffee."

"What did you eat?" Cassie asked.

Leon ignored her question.

"I thought so," she said, accusation in her voice. And then she grabbed his upper arm and tugged on him. "Come on, let's get some breakfast."

Leon got to his feet, not quite sure what to make of the situation. Cassie and he didn't touch each other very much. Not unless it was absolutely necessary. In fact, he was usually hyperaware of not touching her. Probably because he was afraid it would betray the feelings he kept tucked away, the ones he hadn't been able to sort out. And, for whatever reason, Cassie seemed to follow the same guidelines.

That kiss on the cheek last night was just an impulse on her part, likely motivated by her relief at having survived another attack. It was just a kiss on the cheek, after all.

And yet the tug on his arm was something new. Something different. He shook his head slightly and told himself it didn't mean anything as they walked down the hall and into the kitchen where a small TV was tuned to a local early news show.

"Good morning," Sherry called over to them. "I just put on a fresh pot of coffee." To Cassie, she said, "Your dad and Jay ate a while ago. Right now they're out exercising the horses. You two sit down at the table. I'll grab you a couple of mugs and then get started on some breakfast quesadillas for you."

Leon and Cassie sat, and almost immediately Sherry plunked mugs of steaming coffee in front of them. She then fetched half-and-half from the fridge and a sugar dish and spoon from the cabinet. Leon watched as Cassie loaded up her coffee with sugar. Something she oftentimes did when she was feeling especially tired.

"The murder of Jake Wheeler cannot continue to go unsolved."

Cassie and Leon both snapped their attention to the TV screen where the bland drone of the local morning news had suddenly turned into something much more interesting.

"This will not happen," Mayor Al Downing continued. "Not on my watch." He was standing outside city hall, flanked by members of the city council. Three uniformed Idaho state patrol officers stood nearby.

"Oh, the news has been talking about what happened to you driving home from Montana last night," Sherry said, turning from her quesadilla preparations. "You probably want peace and quiet right now. I have the remote right here. I'll turn it off."

"No, wait," Cassie said, holding up her hand. "I want to see it. Would you turn up the volume, please?"

The mayor's statement broadcast live this morning didn't go on much longer. He expressed concern for Cassie's safety, made clear his commitment to make all city resources available to investigators, asked for witnesses to come forth, and announced a boost to the cash reward available for the last five years to anyone who could offer information that would lead to a capture and conviction of Jake's killer.

"Do you see anyone in the background, either walking along the sidewalk or standing and listening, who looks familiar?" Leon asked as the mayor's formal announcement ended and the TV camera pulled back to show a wider scene, which included people headed toward the various public and private downtown offices. It was a truism that criminals were often seen tagging along with investigators as well as showing up at crime scenes. Maybe someone they'd talked to recently would be in the camera shot and unintentionally give them a lead.

"No one looks familiar," Cassie said after taking a sip of coffee, her eyes glued on the TV screen. "But I'm sure this segment will be on the station's website later today. I'll take another look at it."

"Your phone has got to be blowing up with calls and texts by now," Sherry said to Cassie, setting a plate with a quesadilla, salsa and sour cream on the side, in front of each of them. She then grabbed eating utensils and handed a set to each, as well. "If I were you, I'd leave it off all day. You need a break."

"You're right," Cassie said. "People have probably been trying to contact me. I'll go get my phone." She slid out of her chair. "I left it charging in the office last night." She headed down the hallway.

Leon glanced at Sherry, who exhaled loudly and then dropped her chin to her chest for a few seconds before lifting it. "Cassie running for her phone was not what I'd intended." She looked at Leon and shook her head. "I should have known better."

"We've all been there," he said. "You think you're going to manipulate her. But you're not."

Cassie returned with her phone, which had started to power up and was sounding tones and chirps like crazy. She silenced it and set it aside before joining hands with Leon and Sherry to pray a blessing over their meal. After that, Cassie and Leon dug in.

Adam Wheeler had a standing directive about checking phones while eating at the dining room table. The gist of it was that *sometimes* it was necessary to stay on top of incoming calls and messages for various reasons. But most of the time the demands for attention could wait long enough for a person to set the phone aside and either have a meal in peace or enjoy that meal while interacting face-to-face with whoever else was at the table.

Leon didn't know how hungry he was until he took his first bite of the delicious cheese-and-sausage quesadilla, and then he realized he was ravenous.

Cassie was intently focused on her breakfast, too.

When they finished, Sherry cleared the table and Cassie reached for her phone.

"Any calls or messages from the people we talked to in Montana yesterday?" Leon asked.

"I don't see any. There isn't anything from an unidentified number." Cassie scrolled through her phone and then paused. "It looks like Sergeant Bergman called me early this morning."

She set her phone on speaker, tapped the screen and listened to a short message from the detective asking her to call him back.

She disconnected and tapped the phone icon.

After a few rings, Bergman answered. "I understand you and your fellow bounty hunters had an exciting time heading through the pass on the way home last night," he said, forgoing any greeting.

"Yeah," Cassie said heavily. "I'm getting tired of excitement."

Leon watched her closely, concerned this was all becoming too much for her.

"You guys okay?" Bergman asked.

Cassie glanced at Leon. "We could all use a vacation," she said. Her lips lifted in a half smile. "Hawaii, maybe?" She raised her eyebrows at Leon as if asking if he thought that was a good idea.

Leon nodded in return. He'd love to go to Hawaii. Never been. Never traveled beyond the six states that bordered Idaho.

"I could use a trip to Hawaii, myself," Bergman said before exhaling audibly. "So what can you tell me about your trip yesterday? Did you get any leads on Seth?"

Cassie summarized the interactions they'd had. "Maybe we angered someone in Saddleback," she said at the end. "Maybe that's why they shot at us."

"Maybe," Bergman said. "The mayor is once again boosting the profile of your story, especially the angle of finding Jake's killer, and he's increased the reward money. That might get us some helpful information. But it also means we'll have to spend resources on checking out tips that are dead ends."

"I'm focusing my attention on finding Seth right now," Cassie said. "I know the police are trying to track him down, too. Among all the other things you're doing. I told you the specifics about my attempts to find him in Montana yesterday. And you know I struck out. What recent information do *you* have about Seth that you can share with me?"

"Nothing," Bergman said, a hint of frustration in his voice. "I want to talk to him, too. Nobody can find him. He's not using his credit cards. We know his car is still in his garage. Right now, we've got no trail to follow."

"Would you tell me if you did have something?" Cassie asked.

"If I had some information that I couldn't share, I'd tell you 'no comment.' I wouldn't lie to you. Right now, I'm not certain Seth is still alive. Maybe the same people who've been coming after you have already gotten to him."

Cassie looked at Leon and her eyes widened.

"I've got to go," Bergman said. "Keep in touch."

Cassie set her phone on the table after ending the call, tilted her head downward and rubbed her temples. When she looked up, Leon could see that her eyes were red and glistening with unshed tears. "What if what he suggested is true? What if Seth *is* dead? He was my only hope of finding out who killed Jake."

Leon decided to ignore his initial hesitation. He bent closer to Cassie, who was still seated beside him, and wrapped his arm across her shoulders.

To his surprise, she actually leaned into him.

He tilted his head slightly and rested his cheek against the top of her head, closing his eyes for a moment just to savor the feeling of holding her.

"We aren't giving up," he said.

"Of course not."

She sounded indignant, even though Leon could tell she was crying.

He held her a little more tightly and then brushed his lips lightly across the top of her head. He didn't think about it. It just happened.

Cassie's body suddenly stilled and Leon loosened his hold, anticipating that she would pull away.

Instead, she sighed and continued to rest against him. So he kept his arm where it was, wrapped around her shoulders, and redirected his thoughts toward figuring out who was trying to kill her. Determined to stop them before they tried again.

"I know this is all just *stuff*," Cassie said the following day, shortly before noon, as she used her foot to shove aside a small pile of scorched debris at the downtown Rock Solid Bail Bonds office. "I realize that I should focus on being grateful that no *person* was harmed. And I *am* grateful. Very much so. But still, I've spent a lot of time here over the years. And seeing old framed photos and handmade bookcases and even some of the old paper files destroyed feels like I've had part of my past stolen from me."

Cassie looked over at Ramona Orlansky, who was cinching a trash bag full of debris and burned items that were beyond saving.

Ramona glanced at her and offered a sympathetic smile. "I know how you feel. I grew up hanging around my family's diner after school and on weekends. I saw the long hours my parents invested in earning a living. I remember the times when business was slow and my mom and dad had to take out a loan against our house so they could meet payroll." She let go of the bag and brushed her hands on her jeans. "Rock Solid Bail Bonds is the way you earn your living, but it's not just about the money. It's more than that." She nodded. "Believe me, I understand."

Cassie exhaled and felt the sharp pain of loss ease just a little. There truly was something about having a friend who understood what you were going through— even if that friend couldn't change anything—that made a burden feel lighter.

She glanced at Leon, who was disassembling an oversize desk with a side table to make it easier to get it out the door and into the moving truck. At least some of the furniture had survived. The desk, plus a few other salvageable items, would be put into a storage space the insurance company would pay for until the renovations to the office were completed.

A construction crew was scheduled to show up the next day to gut the place and then get started on the repairs.

The pressure was on Cassie to have everything out of the office that she or her dad wanted to keep. Adam's arthritis had been bothering him, so she'd convinced him to stay home and follow up on the research Leon had started rather than help out here. Harry was busy making in-person visits to check in with high-flight-risk bail bond clients. Daisy and Martin had volunteered to head over to Jameson to fetch Leon's truck now that the windshield had been replaced.

"It's hard to believe we'll ever get the charred smell out of here even after we remove all the burned items," Cassie said, looking at the fire-blackened sofa where she'd sat and had countless conversations with her crew and clients over the years. When she'd first met Ramona, they'd sat on that couch, talking, after several thugs had tried to kill Ramona in the dark forest at the edge of a local campground.

"You'll have fun decorating this place after everything's been repaired," Ramona said, wrapping her arm around Cassie for a bolstering side hug before walking over to grab another garbage bag. "Once everything is in place, and the guys spill coffee on your new couch and get pizza grease on your new desktops, it'll feel just like home."

"Hey," Leon called out, "it's not just the guys who make a mess."

"True," Cassie said, managing a laugh. "I have nobody to blame but myself for a desk chair that always smells like French fries."

"I'm throwing out everything in the break room," Ramona said as she headed down the hallway in that direction. "Even the packages of coffee and snacks that are sealed and look like they're okay. It just don't think it's a good idea to keep them."

"Of course," Cassie replied, turning around in the main area of the office for one more good look. Her priority had been to collect everything she'd wanted to keep, and she'd done that. Most of the garbage was now in the big container out back. Just a few more bags to go. Harry would return to the office in an hour or so to help Leon move the few larger pieces of furniture worth saving and repairing. And that would be that.

Leon walked past her with the attachment he'd just removed from the desk he'd been working on and headed for the back door to put it into the truck that would take it to storage. Cassie tracked him with her gaze as he passed by, unable to look away.

He was the same Leon who'd worked for Rock Solid Bail Bonds for four years now. He looked the same. He calmly took care of things just as he always had. But things felt different between the two of them. Like something below the surface had shifted.

Yes, they'd been through some very intense moments these last few days. But they had been in dangerous situations together before. So why was this strange-ness happening *now*? And where did she want it to go? If anywhere? Could this new *attraction* be something temporary that would vanish as soon as they captured whoever had been trying to kill her? And, hopefully, solve Jake's murder?

Her phone pinged. It was probably Harry, texting to let her know he was on his way to the office to help Leon with the furniture. Cassie had offered to help, but Leon had pointed out that she still had some sore joints and muscles that needed healing. And Ramona was busy helping with the cleaning.

She pulled out her phone and glanced at the screen. It was a text from an unknown number. She tapped on it.

You told my coworkers and neighbors you'd offer me anonymity and protection.

Cassie's heart began to pound so hard that the phone shook in her hand. She immediately thought of the cards and messages she'd left with people in Montana. Had one or more of those people passed her message along? Could this truly be Seth?

Seth? Is that you? she texted.

She called out to Leon as he walked into the office and told him what was happening.

A reply text came in.

I need help. Cops and other people are after me.

I can help you, Cassie quickly texted. When and where can I meet you?

It seemed like forever before her phone chimed with a reply.

Tell no one about this. If you comply, I'll be in touch.

"I don't want to wait for him to be 'in touch,'" Cassie said to Leon. "Assuming this is really Seth, he might decide to disappear again."

"Remind him that you can help him," Leon suggested.

I want to help you, Cassie texted. The sooner, the better. Where can we meet? Your choice. I'll come alone.

"You mean you're going to let him *think* you're alone," Leon muttered from beside her.

Five minutes passed and there was no response.

Getting edgy, Cassie decided to call the number connected with the text. It rang multiple times before a robotic voice told her that no voice mailbox had been set up with that phone number.

A couple of minutes passed and she received another text. Leon looked over her shoulder as she read it.

Don't try that again. I'm ditching this phone right now. You'll have to wait.

Great. She might have scared him off by trying to call him.

"He said 'other people' are after him." She turned to Leon, thinking of her phone conversation with Sergeant Bergman yesterday morning. "What if those 'other people' get to him before we do?"

He shrugged. Obviously, he didn't have an answer.

Anxiety turned her breaths shallow.

She didn't want to wait to hear back from Seth. But what other choice did she have?

ELEVEN

An hour after Seth sent the message telling Cassie to wait, he finally sent her a text from a different number with the words she'd been waiting for.

If you keep me safe, I'll tell you all I know. Dangerous people involved.

She and Leon had left the office and were on their way to North Star Ranch when the message arrived. She read it aloud and Leon pulled over to the side of the road.

Why not tell the police all you know? Cassie texted back.

The reply was immediate. No cops!

Cassie didn't want to risk scaring him off for good this time, so she let that topic go, telling herself she'd inform Bergman of what was happening when the time was right. Instead, she asked Seth where and when they could meet.

Will give directions along the way. Start heading toward Montana. Now. Next message in an hour.

Since he was from Montana, it made sense he'd set up a meet in a location familiar to him somewhere in that direction. Gray clouds hung low in the sky. This wasn't the best time to head through the mountain passes, especially since it was already late in the afternoon. But Cassie texted him back to tell him she'd be leaving Stone River shortly. She could be risking another ambush driving through the pass again, but this might be the only opportunity she'd ever have to find out who had murdered her husband. It was a chance she had to take.

Come alone, the next text read.

"No way," Leon said, peering over her arm to read her phone screen.

Not a chance, Cassie shot back in her reply.

Seth couldn't possibly believe she'd agree to traipse to an unknown Montana location by herself. And maybe, by being up-front, she'd earn some credibility points with him.

Long minutes crawled by with no response. She thought she might have blown her chance at meeting with him. But then a message finally came through.

One person with you. NOT A COP! Next message in one hour.

"All right. He says bring one person. I say I'll bring three." She glanced at Leon, who nodded in agreement.

"I'll be the plus one you're admitting to," he said with a slight smile.

She called Martin to tell him and Daisy what was happening. It didn't feel right to put them on the spot by directly asking them to go with her. A personal situation like this wasn't part of their job description. But she was relieved and grateful when they immediately volunteered to accompany her and Leon on the trip.

"I don't know what Seth is going to do or ultimately where he'll send us," Cassie said into her phone with both Daisy and Martin on the other end. "He could have somebody in town watching to see if I have another vehicle traveling with me. Or he might just send me in a big circle that directs me back here to Stone River. So I want you to wait and then head out for Montana thirty minutes after Leon and I leave town, unless you hear otherwise from me. I'll keep you in the loop as I get updated directions from Seth."

Martin and Daisy reminded her to be careful before ending the call.

After gassing up Leon's truck, they hit the highway beneath a cloudburst that seemed determined to travel with them. Roughly an hour later, after they'd passed from Idaho into Montana, another text from Seth arrived.

Look at the next highway road marker and tell me what the number is.

As soon as their headlights hit the next reflective sign in the dusky light beside the highway, Cassie noted the number and texted it to Seth.

He replied with a mile marker number fifteen miles ahead.

Just past this point is a turnoff for an unpaved county road on your left. Turn there. Text me when you've made the turn.

"He's sending us to Rubyville, the ghost town," Leon said after she read aloud the text. "Or the campground that's nearby."

"I've never been to Rubyville," Cassie said. "I've heard of it. Wasn't sure exactly where it was."

"I'm not surprised," Leon said. "I've camped there. It's pretty desolate. Not exactly a tourist attraction."

Cassie made a quick call to update Daisy and Martin. The call seemed to take a long time to go through. When it finally connected, and Daisy answered, her voice was overlaid with static.

"Directions are to turn north on the county road that leads to Rubyville," Cassie said. "Are either of you familiar with the area?"

"I am," Daisy said. She added something else, but her words kept cutting out.

"You're breaking up," Cassie said.

"I said I went hiking around there a couple of times with my family back when I was a kid." Her voice came through a little clearer, but it still sounded choppy. "Man, this is quite a storm. The rain is really coming down," she added, though Cassie had to concentrate to fill in the blanks to understand what she'd said.

"I'll call you when we get further directions," Cassie told her.

The call dropped before she heard Daisy's response.

Cassie turned to Leon. "Tell me about Rubyville and the campground. I've heard the facilities are primitive, so I've never been interested in going. Give me my comfy bed and a hot shower and a decent meal instead, thanks."

"Primitive is the word, all right," he replied. "The campground is just a patch of public land beside the county road that's kept clear of brush so you can pitch a tent. Maybe car camp if you want to. It would be a reasonable place for a fugitive to hide. No one is likely to bother you there. But there's no fresh water spigots, no shower facilities, nothing like that."

"You said you've been camping there. Why would you want to do that? If you want to be all outdoorsy and rugged, why not set up camp in a beautiful section of forest away from it all?"

"Not the best time of my life when I used to go camping out there," he said. "Though I tried to kid myself at the time that I was enjoying myself." Leon sighed heavily. "It's not an area that cops patrol. At least, it wasn't back then. That made it a good place to party with friends. I was stupid. I was lost. Obeying the law, doing the right thing, doing *good*, didn't cross my mind." He shook his head. "I don't claim I was very smart at the time."

"Well, you didn't exactly see good examples growing up," Cassie said. He'd told her a little about his parents, who'd apparently not really been in to parenting.

Leon rubbed the back of his neck. "I'm not making excuses. I knew what I was doing, even though in a lot of ways, I *didn't*."

"You're not that person now," Cassie said. "You're different."

"I know that. I know I'm forgiven. I know I've been redeemed. And I am truly grateful for that. More than words can say. 'Thank You, Lord' never feels like enough. But I do pray those words at least once every day. Usually a lot more often than that."

"He knows what's in your heart," Cassie said. "And that's what matters."

"I made a lot of stupid decisions that impacted my future and will continue to impact my future," Leon added. "Those realities aren't going to go away."

"All I know is that every step you've taken in your life has made you the man you are right now. And there's no other man I'd rather have by my side," she said.

Hearing those words come out of her mouth made Cassie's stomach flutter and she felt a twinge of panic. Because they were *true*. But she hadn't meant to give voice to them. And acting on them would be impossible. Leon was her *employee*. She couldn't, and wouldn't, play games with that. Working for her was his livelihood, and she didn't want him to feel like he was risking that. Not for her. Not for anybody. *She* certainly wouldn't want to ever be put in that situation.

The moment hung in the air between them, heavy, like something bold needed to be said. And Cassie, who liked to think she had some backbone, chickened out and changed the subject. "So did you hike over to Rubyville and check out the actual ghost town when you were camping or partying nearby?"

"Yeah. It's mostly a few abandoned houses and storefronts and a church. Plus some old barns and stables and storage buildings. Somebody found gold in a nearby creek in the late 1800s and people hustled here from all over the West thinking they'd strike it rich. A few of them made some money. The town had nearly a thousand residents at one point. But after about five years, the gold played out. There was a harsh winter that, sadly, some of the residents didn't survive. People left as soon as the passes cleared and, within a couple of years, the town was abandoned."

"Sounds like a good place to explore sometime. But right now, it looks like Seth is hiding there. And I'm hoping we can talk to him. Find out who killed Jake. Finally get everything that's been happening resolved."

A short time later, they spotted the road Seth had told them to watch for. Leon slowed and made the turn. Cassie sent her text to Seth.

We just made the turnoff from the highway.

Her heart rate sped up at the thought that she was finally about to talk face-to-face with the man who apparently knew the details of Jake's murder.

Leon's recently repaired truck rocked from side to side after he left the even asphalt of the highway and turned onto the unpaved county road. It was still raining, the road was muddy, and Cassie thought it a very good thing that Leon drove around on big, fat, deeply treaded tires.

Her phone pinged and she looked at the screen to see the newest text from Seth. Or at least the person who was leading her to believe he was Seth. This could be a trap laid by the people trying to kill her. She'd had to consider that from the moment she'd received the first message.

She read the text to Leon. "'You're going to see a maple tree on the right and just beyond it is a narrow dirt road. Turn there.'"

"Yeah, he's taking us off the county road that leads to the campground and having us take the old road toward Rubyville," Leon said. He made the turn, leaving the county road to drive up what was little more than an overgrown path with deep grooves worn into it, likely originally put there by wagon wheels.

"Keep an eye out for fresh tire tracks. Like, from a vehicle with an internal combustion engine and not one drawn by mules," Cassie said.

"Copy that," Leon replied. "Though the rain has probably washed away any tracks Seth left behind if he's been here for a while."

Cassie tapped her phone screen to call Daisy to tell them it was confirmed they were heading to Rubyville. The call went through, but again the reception was staticky. It sounded like Daisy said something about a rockslide and the road being blocked.

Cassie repeatedly tried to explain where they were, but the call obviously wasn't clear on Daisy's end, either. Eventually, Cassie was fairly sure she'd made her point. She believed Daisy had told her that Martin thought he could make his way around the rockslide, but that they would be delayed.

When the call dropped, Cassie sent Daisy a text asking for an estimate on how long she and Martin thought they would be.

Martin doesn't think it will take too long. Hold off the meeting for an hour. We should be there to back you up by then.

"If we can hold off for an hour, we will," Cassie muttered to Leon after she'd read the text to him.

The rain slackened and the bumpy road curved around a cluster of towering Ponderosa pines before straightening. In the beams of the truck's headlights, Cassie could see two rows of dilapidated wooden buildings facing each other from opposite sides of the street. The road she and Leon were driving along continued between the rows of grayed buildings then dead-ended a few yards ahead where a wide turnabout had been worn into the ground.

Leon stopped just before they reached the faded buildings.

"Do you see anybody, or maybe a parked vehicle anywhere?" Cassie asked.

"No," Leon replied. "But I feel like a sitting duck just waiting here." He turned off the truck's headlights and interior lights.

Cassie gave her eyes a few moments to adjust to the deepening twilight. Though the cloud cover made things dimmer, it wasn't full night yet. The winds that buffeted the truck, rocking it slightly, were also breaking up the clouds overhead. It had been predicted to be a fast-moving storm.

Cassie rolled down her window to listen. "Maybe we got here ahead of him. Maybe he's back where we turned off the highway, watching to see if we brought cops with us."

"That's what I would do if I were him," Leon said. "Why don't you let him know we're here?" he added.

Cassie's phone pinged just as she started to compose a text. It was an incoming message.

I see you.

Gooseflesh rippled across the surface of her skin as she quickly looked up. "He sees us," she said to Leon. Then she looked around, trying to peer into the shadows of the surrounding forest and the tilting, aging buildings. Of course, the windows had long been broken. Doors were missing and, in some cases, entire walls had collapsed. But there were still places for someone to hide.

What if this wasn't really Seth meeting them here? Or what if he wasn't now contacting them because he was afraid and needed help? What if he—or whomever had sent the texts—had drawn them here to kill them?

Another message came through.

Drive forward to the turnabout.

"I think we've let Seth control the situation long enough," Leon said after she relayed the message. "He must be in contact with at least a couple of neighbors or coworkers since he knows we're looking for him, but other than that, he's stayed out of sight. I believe he really is scared. The guy hasn't got a criminal record other than driving under the influence. It's possible he's a brilliant mastermind intent on hurting us, but I think it's more likely he needs our help."

"You're right." She sent Seth a text.

Show yourself.

Three minutes dragged slowly by before the reply came.

Meet me at the old dry goods store. Building closest to turnabout.

"Pull up to that building," Cassie said.

"Don't let him talk you into going inside to meet with him," Leon said dubiously as he started to inch the truck slowly forward. "We shouldn't do much of anything until Daisy and Martin get here to back us up."

"There's no telling how long it will take them. Just because Martin wants to make his way around the rockslide quickly doesn't mean he'll be able to. Turn your headlights back on," Cassie said when the truck was alongside the dry goods store.

"Step into the headlights with your hands up. When it's safe, I'll step out to talk with you." Cassie spoke the words as she texted them, so that Leon would know what she was planning.

"That's a good start," Leon said cautiously.

"I want you to stay inside the truck where you can see everything," she said. "Keep the interior lights turned off in case he decides to take a shot at you. And make sure your phone doesn't light you up." They'd done plenty of stakeouts and surveillance in the nighttime hours, so her last two directives weren't really necessary. But she'd wanted to remind Leon to be careful. She didn't want him hurt because of her drive to know who'd murdered Jake and why.

The rain had turned into a slight drizzle.

"Let's keep the windows rolled down and cut the engine so we can hear anyone approaching," Cassie said.

Leon complied.

While they waited for Seth to show himself, Cassie shifted her view back and forth from the windshield to the side mirror in case someone was trying to sneak up on them from behind. Finally, ten yards in front of the truck, she saw a figure walk out from the narrow passage between the dry goods store and the nearly collapsed storage building beside it.

Seth.

He'd cut his hair shorter than it was in his booking photo. And he'd bleached it from medium brown to an almost-white blond. He appeared noticeably skinnier than he had in the photo, too. But there he was, look-ing at the truck's headlights, squinting.

Cassie reached for her handgun on the seat beside her, leaned forward, and tucked it into the waistband at the small of her back.

"Be careful," Leon said as she slowly opened the door and slid out.

"Right," Cassie said without looking at him. She kept her gaze locked on the person who could finally answer her questions.

"Seth Tatum," Cassie called out as she stepped closer to the young man. He looked terrified, and younger than his twenty-three years. "I've been waiting a long time to talk to someone who knows what happened to my husband."

"And I've been waiting a long time to get out from under this," he answered, clasping his hands together in front of him and sounding genuinely overwrought. As Cassie drew closer, she could see the dark circles around his eyes and the exhaustion evident in his slumped pos-ture. He started to drop his hands.

"Wait!" Cassie said. "Put your hands up. I'm going to pat you down really quick. Make sure you aren't armed."

He didn't resist as she frisked him. She didn't find any weapons on him. "Okay, you can put your hands down," she said.

He dropped his hands.

Cassie took in a deep breath and slowly blew it out. Her stomach tightened as she anticipated what she was about to hear from the man in front of her. "Did you kill my husband?" she asked. That could be the real rea-son why he was scared and in hiding. He was afraid he was about to be caught and charged with murder. And maybe there was a small spark of decency in him that made him feel guilty for what he'd done.

"I did not." Even though the rain had slackened, he was soaked and his T-shirt clung to his body. He'd apparently been outside in the elements for a while. Maybe he'd been hanging around Rubyville waiting for her arrival. Or he could have hiked over from the camping area Leon had mentioned.

"If you didn't kill my husband, who did?" Cassie willed herself to remain calm even though, at the moment, talking with this man about Jake's murder made her heart feel like it was cracking into pieces. Maybe Seth was lying. Maybe he'd intended to confess and then changed his mind.

"Who is with you?" Seth asked, lifting his chin in the direction of the truck.

"One of my bounty hunters," Cassie said. "Leon Bragg."

"Who else?"

"No one else."

"Before I tell you what I know, I need you to tell me how you can protect me. Because when word gets out, well, it's going to be big."

Cassie bit back her impatience. Of course he would want to arrange some sort of deal to protect his own hide. Pretty much every fugitive she'd ever caught had wanted to negotiate with her.

She quickly thought about what she could offer in terms of protection, imagining that someone with extensive criminal resources like drug supplier Stefan Kasparov might be looking to permanently silence Seth. She could provide a safe location where he could hide. Plus, at least one personal bodyguard. Namely, herself.

But before she could answer him, a loud *crack* tore through the quiet of the evening, followed by several more.

Rifle shots.

Leon turned off the truck's headlights, casting the center of the ghost town into darkness.

Cassie and Seth both ducked down. She drew her gun, grabbed Seth's arm and pulled him with her as she started running. There was no way she would let Seth get away from her until she had her answers.

Cassie headed for the passage between the buildings—the same one Seth had used—trying to get to the back of the dry goods store and hopefully out of striking distance of the flying bullets.

Meanwhile, the truck's engine roared to life. Leon flicked the headlights back on, the brightness appearing in Cassie's peripheral vision, as he quickly backed up, swung the vehicle around and illuminated the forest in the direction of the shooter.

Cassie didn't dare stop to watch, but from the corner of her eye she thought she'd seen two figures moving among the trees. The shooting had stopped, but she wasn't foolish enough to think the attack was over.

"Where's your vehicle?" she demanded of Seth as soon as they dropped down behind the back of the dry goods store. Several boards were missing from the building and what was left didn't look especially strong, but at least it offered some kind of barrier between them and the shooters.

"My truck is parked at the campground a couple of miles from here," he said, confirming both Leon's theory that he'd been hiding at the campground, and Cassie's assumption that he must have obtained a secondary vehicle since his registered car was still parked in the garage at his house.

Crack! More shots sounded in the direction they'd just run from. Only this time, they ended with the dull *thunk* sound of metal striking metal. And then she heard bullets striking glass.

The gunmen were firing at Leon in the truck. She wondered if these were the same men who'd pursued them in the forest back in Stone River. If so, they were very good at tracking. And she and Leon—and Seth—were in imminent danger.

Lord, please protect Leon and guide us all, she quickly prayed, forcing her thoughts away from her fear before it could paralyze her.

"Who's shooting at us?" she demanded of Seth.

He was hunkered down beside her, terror-filled eyes visible in the ambient light. She still had a grip on his arm, but he wasn't acting like he wanted to get away from her.

"I don't know who it is." He practically wailed the words.

"You're lying. How could you not know?" She shook his arm. "*Who killed my husband*? Who is afraid of being exposed? Is it Kasparov? Or people hired by him?"

Seth shook his head with several short, tight movements. "I'm not saying. If they catch us, and I haven't told you anything, then maybe they won't kill me."

"At least one of the two thugs shooting at us has *got* to be the person who killed my husband," Cassie said. "I think they intend to shut you up. And they want to shut me up, too, because they think I know something."

"No," Seth said firmly. "You're wrong. The person

who killed your husband could not possibly be one of those shooters."

Cassie huffed out her impatience. Demanding that he explain himself would only end up with her being dragged back into another of his frustrating conversational circles and she didn't have time for that. What she needed to do was to focus on Leon, making sure that he was okay. A few minutes had passed since she'd last heard gunfire, which could be a bad sign. It didn't seem likely that the two shooters would have already given up and run away. Maybe one of their shots had hit the mark and they'd been able to silence Leon.

Her heart hammered in her chest and her blood ran cold at the thought of Leon being harmed. He'd become such a big part of her life. And not only because she worked with him nearly every day in a dangerous profession.

Somehow her sorrow-filled life had grown around him. Like one of the old trees she'd seen in the forest that had been split by a lightning strike, or charred by a wildfire, and yet the tree had not only survived, but had begun to grow in new directions, appearing to thrive once again despite the damage.

Around her, Cassie could hear rainwater dripping from tree branches and dribbling from the eaves of the roofs. The increasing breeze caused the surrounding tree branches and boards of the old buildings to moan and squeak. She looked around, listening intently for the sound of footsteps. Or the sound of someone loading a round into a rifle just before they fired at her.

She didn't hear anything that concerned her. For the moment, at least, it seemed as if she and Seth were alone. Still, she didn't dare put away her gun.

"Don't go anywhere," she whispered to Seth as she let go of his arm to reach for her phone.

He immediately took off running.

"You're not getting away!" She leaped on him, shoving his face down into the mud. Before he could gather his wits, she was already standing on his back. She might not be a very big woman—certainly not as tall or as heavy as Seth—but she did have a pretty good idea of where to press her boot heel so it would inflict the most pain if he tried to get away from her.

"Okay, okay." His voice was muffled as he tried to speak around the mud. "I'm sorry, I won't do that again. Let me up."

Cassie didn't believe him, so she didn't move. Meanwhile, she was disheartened when she glanced at her phone and there was no message or missed call notice from Leon.

She *had* to know that he was all right. And they obviously needed to meet up.

You ok? she finally texted, wary of the possibility that if the bad guys had managed to overpower him, they would have his phone and would likely try to trick her into revealing her location.

Several seconds passed with no response.

She stepped off Seth, grabbed his arm and pulled him to his feet. "If you try to run, I will push your face into the mud again," she whispered fiercely. "And after that, I will use you as a human shield if there is any more shooting. Do you understand me?"

She wouldn't *really* use him as a human shield. But he didn't know that.

Seth's eyes grew wide and he nodded vigorously. "Yes, ma'am."

Cassie triple-checked that the sound notifications were turned off on her phone. And then, phone in one hand and gun in the other, she started walking along the back of the dry goods store with Seth beside her. She headed in the direction she'd last seen Leon's truck, remaining hidden behind the buildings. She half expected Seth to take off running again, but he didn't.

Once she got closer to the truck, she would look for footprints in the mud and then figure out which direction to search for Leon next based on what she saw. She and Leon had found each other in the wilderness while being tracked by deadly gunmen before. They could do it again.

She'd just stepped past a narrow gap between two weather-beaten buildings when she heard the sound of a footstep. And then felt the cold metal of a gun muzzle pressed against the side of her neck.

TWELVE

Leon scanned the moonlit ghost town, his gaze sweeping across the aged, creaking buildings as he searched for movement or maybe the flicker of a shadow.

The shooters knew what they were doing. Leon had been able to discern that there were two of them, but that was all he knew. Because, after initially opening fire, they'd vanished.

Cassie, where are you? His heart pounded as he stayed hidden behind the corner of the half-collapsed stable. From there he had a fairly good view of the abandoned town. He was tempted to boldly step out and start looking for her. Anticipating that she might be hurt or in trouble made his heart feel like ground glass in the center of his chest.

This wasn't the first time he'd feared for her safety, and he knew how to force himself to resist the instinct to act, to take a breath and try to be smart instead. He couldn't afford to take any risks that might get him killed or incapacitated, because that would leave Cassie completely on her own. Facing at least two gunmen intent on killing her. Plus Seth Tatum, who was a completely unknown factor for Leon right now. There was no telling which side that guy was on. Maybe the meeting had been a setup from the beginning.

Leon had last seen Cassie when she'd darted past the old dry goods store with Seth in tow. He focused his gaze in that direction now, hoping that the gunmen hadn't also seen her there. And if they had seen her, she'd hopefully moved on to somewhere else by now. He steadied his breathing and listened. The buffeting breeze had kicked up again, shaking the raindrops from needles on the pine trees and increasing the volume of the low moaning sound the branches made as they swayed. That made it hard to hear anything.

He glanced down at his silenced phone. He had one flickering bar, indicating minimal, unreliable connection. Great. She could be messaging or calling but the communication wasn't making it through. Or she could be in a situation where she couldn't reach out to him. Or where it might be dangerous for her to use her phone.

Where were the other bounty hunters?

He tucked his gun into his waistband and quickly composed a message to Martin. Need help NOW! and hit Send while silently praying. *Please, Lord, let this go through.* He was counting on his colleagues to at least be close to the ghost town by now. If so, they'd be quicker to respond than the cops, so he'd sent his plea for help to them first. He was about to call 9-1-1 when he heard what he thought was the sound of a dog barking. And then he realized it was the short, barking laugh of a man.

Goose bumps rippled over Leon's skin. It was likely one of the gunmen laughing. And the laugh of a bad guy was *never* a good sign.

He shoved his phone back into his pocket and

grabbed his gun. Then he started a crouching run across the weed-choked road that divided the town, heading toward the long building that used to be a boardinghouse.

The years Leon had spent partying in the past felt like wasted time to him now. But at the moment, because those choices had led him to spend hours wandering through the ruined old buildings of Rubyville, they were proving helpful. He knew the layout of the ghost town. He knew the good places to hide. He knew that the unsettling laughter he'd heard had come from behind the single-story building beside the boarding house. And he knew that if he went into the boarding house, he could move through one of the sections of missing wall and slip into the building next to it. From there, he'd be able to see what was happening in the back. Hopefully, he'd be able to see Cassie.

He took a quick glance over his shoulder. There was no sign of anyone behind him. And no one had taken a shot at him, so the gunmen were likely together. They obviously knew he was in the proximity of the ghost town, somewhere. They'd seen him drive his truck to the edge of the surrounding forest, trying to catch them. Most likely, their first priority was to kidnap or kill Cassie. Then they would come after Leon.

Not if he found them first.

He made his way through the boarding house to the wall adjoining the neighboring building, his movements aggravatingly slow as he navigated the few floorboards still in place and the exposed dirt where the others had rotted away. He crossed into the connecting building and dropped down into the corner beside a window where the glass had been broken out long ago. He could hear a man talking, his voice unfamiliar. But then he heard that barking laugh again.

Doing his best to stay out of sight, Leon took a quick look out the window. What he saw sent his heart tumbling to his feet.

Cassie sat in the mud, her legs folded beneath her. Seth sat in the mud to her left, also with his legs folded beneath him. A man, standing close to Cassie's right, held a rifle pointed at her head. Cassie's gun was tucked into his waistband. A second man, the one with the barking laugh, stood several feet in front of them where he moved around impatiently and then finally stopped. He also had a rifle, which he kept pointed in the general direction of the two captives.

Both gunmen wore masks. But their stances, and the way they held their rifles, seemed familiar. And then Leon thought of the men tracking him and Cassie through the forest and shooting at them when this all began six days ago.

Leon had tracked a lot of people in his career. He'd learned how to identify people not just by looking at their face or their clothes, but also by observing the way they stood and moved. Based on their skill in eluding Leon and capturing Cassie, plus their stances and movements, he was sure that these two were the same men. Of course, he'd considered the possibility from the moment he'd identified that there were two of them. But now he was sure of it.

"Who *are* you?" he heard Cassie demand of the barking-laugh man. "Why do you want to kill me?"

Despite the life-threatening situation, she defiantly raised her chin. Admiration for the woman mixed with gut-wrenching fear for her life set Leon's emotions spinning. She turned her head to look at the gunman beside her, and Leon could see a swipe of mud across her cheek. It did not look like she'd fallen in the mud. It looked like one of the men had struck her.

Anger, hot and acidic, began to rise in Leon's gut.

"You are a troublesome loose end," Barking-Laugh Man said to her. "You, too," he added, turning to Seth. "All you had to do was keep your mouth shut. And you couldn't even do that."

Seth dropped his chin to his chest, looking defeated.

Leon moved away from the window, toward the closest corner inside the building. He *had* to do something. If he waited too long, the gunman might kill Cassie before he acted. But if he barreled into the middle of things right this minute, they could start shooting and that could lead to her instant death. *Where were Martin and Daisy?* They should have been here by now. And if they couldn't get around the rockslide, they should have called the cops and alerted them about Cassie's meeting with Seth.

He was wary of exposing his phone's screen in the darkness, where the light could shine through the spaces between the weathered boards of the building and give away his location, ruining everything. But he took the chance, ducking away from the window frame and holding the phone close to his chest to look for a message from Martin or Daisy.

Nothing.

He needed to call 9-1-1 and pray that the call would go through.

Before he tapped the screen, he took another quick look through the window to make certain the situation with Cassie and the gunmen was relatively stable. And then he heard the grinding sound of a vehicle, most likely a truck, making its way up the rutted trail leading into Rubyville.

Martin and Daisy.

Leon tapped his phone to make a quick call to tell Martin where he was, and to plan how the three of them would take down these thugs and rescue Cassie. But before the call could connect, the vehicle roared up closer to the building he was hiding in. How had they known to come to this specific building? Cassie must have somehow managed to let Martin and Daisy know where she was being held. Probably sent a quick text before she'd been captured by the criminals. Leave it to her to keep a cool head and get things done no matter the situation.

Leon quickly tried to connect with Martin again, but the call wouldn't go through. The ghost town was built at the base of a towering rock outcropping, so the phone issues weren't a complete surprise. Especially with the stormy, unstable weather. But that didn't make it any less frustrating.

He gave up on talking to Martin and Daisy, shoved the phone into his pocket, and figured that as soon as the bounty hunters walked around the corner of the building, he would jump out from his hiding place. He knew he could count on Cassie to spring into action to help save herself.

He heard two truck doors open and shut. He rose to peer out the window again. The gunman by Cassie's side kept an eye on her. The other one, the guy with the barking laugh who seemed to be the person in charge, glanced toward the corner of the building where approaching footsteps could be heard striking the exposed rock in the muddy ground.

Leon drew a breath, gripping the gun in his hand and tensing his body as he readied to jump through the open window frame. With no coordinated plan of attack in place, it was a good thing that he, Martin and Cassie had worked together so much that they could anticipate each other's moves. And from the relatively short time he'd spent working with Daisy, he'd seen ample evidence that she knew how to deal with a dangerously unpredictable situation, too.

He heard the footsteps moving closer and prepared to move. Just as the steps reached the corner of the building, he jumped out the window.

The new arrivals *weren't* Martin and Daisy. They were two more men. Both wearing masks, just like the original two.

Cassie was on her feet in an instant, kicking the man beside her in the gut while his attention was drawn to the new arrivals.

The startled newcomers were still trying to make sense of the scene in front of them when Leon quickly grabbed Cassie's arm and hustled her toward the nearby forest. He didn't much care about Seth's safety. He was the reason Cassie and Leon were there and their lives were in danger. But as Leon and Cassie took off running in the darkness, Seth ran with them.

Bam! Bam!

Leon planned to use the surrounding dark forest for cover until they could get to his truck. Then they'd jump in it and get out of town. If any of the assailants had night-vision or heat-detection equipment, there would not be much time before they were caught.

When they were as close to the truck as they could get, they broke cover and ran for it.

Bam! Bam! Two more shots. But they didn't sound like they were being fired near Cassie and Leon. It sounded like they were coming from behind the boarding house.

Were the gunmen searching for Cassie and Leon in the wrong direction? Maybe firing a few shots to try to scare them and flush them out? It didn't seem likely. But Leon didn't have time to figure out what they were doing. He just needed to get Cassie and himself out of Rubyville and away from danger.

"Are you all right?" he asked Cassie as they got closer to his truck. It was the first chance he'd had to ask her.

"No!" she snapped. "I'm not all right. I'm *furious*."

That meant that, physically, she was probably okay.

He heard several more shots from behind the boardinghouse, which prompted all three runners to move faster as Seth continued to keep up. The brisk breeze stirred the clouds overhead, allowing them clearer sight lines as they ran, but also making them easier targets.

With that little bit of added moonlight, Leon could now see that his truck was tilted at an odd angle. *Please, no.* As they got closer to it, the flat rear tire was clearly visible. As was the handle of the hunting knife sticking out of it.

He heard gunshots again. Only, they were louder now. Closer. And then he caught the sound of bullets hitting the ground not far away. Somebody was shooting at them.

Not willing to risk taking a look back to see which of the four possible thugs was doing the shooting, Leon pressed Cassie in front of him and shouted, "Head for the woods!"

They ran as fast as they could, with Seth doggedly staying with them. That worried Leon. Because even though Seth didn't *appear* to be friends with any of the gunmen, it could all be a ruse. He could be keeping up with Cassie and Leon, only to turn them over to the shooters when it might work to his advantage.

"You told me you had a truck at the campground," Cassie said to Seth after they'd put some distance between themselves and the shooters and dropped down behind a fallen tree to catch their breaths. "Take us to it."

"I left it parked not far from here." Though Seth was noticeably younger than Cassie and Leon, he seemed much more winded from running and kept taking shallow, panted breaths. "I bought an old pickup with a camper shell. Cheap. Paid cash. Gave the guy a fake name for the transfer of registration. Been living in it ever since."

Cassie was ready to get up and run toward the campground and Seth's camper. Leon, who was propped up and looking over the fallen tree watching for pursuers, was obviously ready to run again, too. But Seth was still gasping, each intake of air starting to make wheezing sounds.

"If you're asthmatic, you need to take a hit of your inhaler," Cassie said.

Seth shook his head. "I do have asthma, but I didn't dare go to the pharmacy for a prescription refill. Too afraid they would find me if I did that."

"Who are *they*?" Cassie demanded, tired of waiting for the answers he'd promised to give her. "What's going on? Why do they want to kill me? Did they kill my husband?" The questions fired out of her like projectiles and she couldn't stop them.

So much of her life—of life in general—had not made much sense to her since the day Jake had been murdered. Somehow she'd managed to learn how to get through her days with all the unanswered questions hovering in the back of her mind. But then Seth had hinted about things he knew while he was in that jail cell with Phil. And as a result, all of those demoralizing, unanswered questions that had been quieted for a while were now back in the forefront of Cassie's thoughts throughout the day. Every day. Getting in the way as she continued to try to process her grief. Keeping her from moving forward with her life.

Instead of responding to her questions, Seth turned away.

Frustrated, Cassie reached out, wrapped her hand around his chin and turned his head so he was looking at her. *"Answer me,"* she demanded, letting go so he could talk.

"No!" His expression turning cagey. "I know you'll keep me alive so you can get your answers. So you get me to safety first, and then you'll find out what you want to know."

Cassie wanted to punch him in the face. But she didn't do it.

The relative quiet of the forest was broken by the sounds of snapping twigs and footfalls, someone obviously moving quickly in their direction. After only a few seconds Cassie realized it was likely *two* people.

But which two? The first pair of gunmen or the second? Did it make any difference?

No, at the moment it didn't matter. All four gunmen were dangerous. She, Leon and Seth needed to get moving again and quickly make their way to Seth's truck.

"Let's go," Leon said, standing while he held his gun pointed toward the unseen people moving in their direction.

Cassie sprang up. Seth was slow to move, so she grabbed the front of his shirt and pulled him to his feet. "I know it's hard to run when you can't breathe very well, but you have to try," she said, forcing herself to display a compassion she didn't really feel. *Blessed are the merciful, for they shall obtain mercy.* At the very least, she should probably get her facts straight before she dumped all of her anger and frustration on Seth.

They headed for the campground. The underbrush in the forest was thick with small saplings, exposed roots from bigger trees, vines and grasses claiming much of the ground. Leon tried to stay slightly behind Cassie and Seth to stave off the gunmen, who sounded like they were closing in on them. But Cassie dropped back to his side as soon as she realized what he was doing. "You know the way to the campground, so you should probably take lead," she said to him. Then she gestured at Seth. "I don't trust this guy to take us in the right direction."

They were navigating as best they could in the darkness when bullets started to ping off the trees surrounding them. That got them running faster, until Seth stumbled over something and face-planted onto the ground. Cassie and Leon slowed and turned, waiting for him to get up and resume running. But he didn't.

Instead he pushed himself up partway but then just sat there, his shoulders slumped, his face downturned, looking defeated.

With a huff of impatience, Cassie hurried back to him, Leon close by her side, the two intent on getting Seth back on his feet and moving again.

"We've got to keep going," she whispered loudly as she approached him.

Too late, she saw the glint of gunmetal in the thick forest barely ten feet away. Two masked gunmen stepped forward, their weapons aimed at Cassie and Leon.

At such a close range, Leon didn't dare move to take aim at them. They'd be dead before he could fire a single round.

"You did this on purpose!" Cassie snapped at Seth.

He shook his head. "No," he said forlornly, "I didn't."

"You had to know we'd catch up with you eventually," one of the gunmen said in an eerily calm tone. "No reason to blame poor Seth." Both shooters had pulled up the bottoms of their masks so the lower half of their faces were visible. They'd probably done it so they could breathe easier while running. But with the top halves of their faces covered and the darkness and shadows, Cassie couldn't see who they were.

"Who *are* you?" she demanded, frustrated because the voice of the man who'd spoken to her sounded familiar, but she couldn't quite place it. One thing she knew for certain, this was *not* one of the men who'd pointed a gun at her just a few minutes ago when she'd been forced to sit in the mud, Seth beside her.

So where were the first two gunmen? *Who* were they? What was going on?

She heard Leon move beside her. One of the gunmen quickly flicked on a bright rectangular light that looked like the flashlight app from a phone. Cassie turned her face from the glare and saw that Leon had moved his gun so that it was aimed at the man who'd just spoken to Cassie.

"Drop your weapon or die," the second gunman said to Leon.

"Now is as good a time as any to shoot them," the first gunman said. The one whose voice sounded familiar to Cassie.

"Drop your gun *now*, or we'll shoot both of you," the second gunman said when Leon didn't obey his command.

No! Cassie thought. *She* was the one they were after. Not Leon. It was her fault Leon was in danger. And it was time he looked out for himself instead of looking out for her. He had to make it through this attack or execution or whatever it was, even if Cassie didn't. She couldn't stand the thought of anything happening to him because she loved him.

Loved him. Not like a buddy she worked with. Not like some kind of stand-in for her late husband. Not like some friend she'd grown attached to because she hadn't had a romantic life for years. No, *she loved Leon Bragg.* As in wanting a future together with him. She was through with finding reasons to keep her emotional distance from him.

What a time and place to realize that.

Too late, it seemed.

"Let him go," Cassie said. "I'm the one you're after. Your masks are still on. We don't know who you are.

You can let him go. He won't be able to describe you to the police."

Cassie heard a sound behind her. She thought it might be Leon moving forward to argue with her. It wasn't.

A flash of something metallic flew through the air toward the two gunmen. The phone-flashlight was suddenly on its side in a tuft of grass, illuminating the hilt of a knife sticking out of the second gunman's leg. He took an unsteady step and tumbled to the ground.

Cassie felt a rush of movement beside her as Leon darted past to tackle the first gunman. There was the brief sound of a scuffle. And then she heard a voice.

"Leon, I really do think you could have had a pro football career." Martin stepped into the light and hurried over to help Leon secure the two gunmen.

"Hey, Cassie, I'm coming up behind you," Daisy called out from the darkness. "I don't want to startle you."

Cassie turned on shaky legs to see the bounty hunter coming out of the forest. Meanwhile, Seth was still sitting on the ground where he'd fallen after he'd tripped. It didn't look like he'd moved an inch.

"Nice knife-throwing skills," Cassie said to Daisy.

"Thank you," Daisy replied. "I pulled the knife out of Leon's tire. Kind of an odd place for him to keep it, don't you think?" she teased before wrapping her arms around Cassie for a hug. "You okay?" she asked.

Cassie choked back a sob of relief that had started to rise in her throat. "I will be."

"I'm sorry it took us so long to get here," Daisy said. "The rockslide was more extensive than we realized. And the phone reception was tricky. When we got here and saw Leon's truck, we knew something was wrong and called the cops. It took a couple of tries but we finally got through. We called them again when we found the bodies."

"Bodies?"

"Yeah, two guys dressed in blackout. Like your friends here." She gestured toward the two men who were now sitting on the ground, hands behind their backs, and Leon and Martin standing guard.

"Were they wearing their masks?" Cassie asked. "Could you see their faces?"

"Their masks were pulled up. Neither one looked familiar. Both had been fatally shot."

"Well, now I can look to see who these two are," Cassie said, heading over to the assailants.

She reached the second gunman first. The guy who'd threatened Leon. She could see a moderate amount of blood on his thigh, and the knife on the grass beside him. She kicked it out of his reach. It appeared that the blade hadn't gone too deep. She pulled up his mask and looked into the scowling face of Kirk Downing.

That made absolutely no sense. She stared at him for a moment, stunned. Why would the mayor's son want her dead?

And then she swept her gaze to the other gunman as her thoughts rapidly shifted to the recent news conferences centered around the recovery of her husband's killer. She thought of this gunman's familiar voice and shook her head slightly. He couldn't possibly be who she now thought he was. She yanked off the mask and found herself staring at the face of Stone River's mayor, Al Downing.

Al Downing?

Nearly impossible to believe. Yet Seth's fear of being

in Stone River and his refusal to trust the police now made sense.

Cassie asked the mayor point-blank, "Did you kill my husband?"

He set his mouth firmly and refused to answer.

"He did kill your husband!" Seth leaped to his feet and moved closer to Cassie and the two Downing men.

"Shut up, Seth," the mayor's son said.

Seth shook his head. "No!" There was a strength in his tone that hadn't been there before.

"Mayor Al was just about to be elected to his first term in office when it all happened," Seth told Cassie. "Kirk was making money dealing drugs back then. Your husband was on the task force trying to combat drug trafficking in town and he saw Kirk making a transaction with Stefan Kasparov, the drug supplier. It was in the parking lot of the big truck stop near the Stuart Street exit."

Seth spewed the words rapidly, as though he couldn't get his explanation out fast enough. "Kirk and Stefan were in the parking lot conducting business, when the trooper, your husband, drove up. He got out of his car, pulled out his phone and looked like he was videotaping everything in front of him.

"Kirk panicked, because there he was with a known drug supplier. He told his dad what had happened. Old Al's plans as mayor included making money for himself and his friends. He couldn't let those plans be ruined because his son was stupid enough to conduct illegal business in such a visible, public place. They decided they needed to kill Jake before he could study the video, recognize Kirk, and possibly cost Al the election. And they got a couple of friends, outdoorsmen who could track and kill the trooper, to help them in return for some of the under-the-table money Al would be making once he got into office."

So the two "outdoorsmen" friends must have been the men who'd tracked Cassie and Leon in the forest, and kidnapped Cassie, and set up the ambush. And they were possibly the same two who'd thrown the explosives into the bail bonds office.

"I heard and saw it all, because I'd been friends with Kirk since we were little kids," Seth continued, still wheezing a little. "I hung around at the Downing house all the time. It was like I was part of the family and they didn't bother to hide any of their plans from me." He shook his head. "I was barely eighteen at the time. And too scared to know what to do or how to get out of the whole mess."

"You're weak," Kirk said, his tone sharp with disgust. "You were always weak. Becoming friends with you was the worst mistake I ever made."

"No! It was the worst mistake *I* ever made," Seth shot back. And then he started to cry. "I'm sorry," Seth said to Cassie. "I should have figured out a way to stop them. I should have gone to the police, but I didn't. I don't know what else to say, except I'm sorry."

For a moment or two, the forest was quiet except for the sounds of Seth's sobbing.

Cassie stared at the two Downing men. At least she finally had an answer. She didn't have the exact details, like who'd specifically shot Jake, and she wasn't sure she ever wanted to know. But at least now her husband's ultimately senseless death had some kind of narrative around it. She finally had what she'd wanted: an explanation. And she didn't feel a sense of release or relief now that she had it. All she felt was numb.

Cassie heard the wail of police sirens followed by the grinding sounds of vehicles climbing up the rough road into Rubyville. She didn't know how to react. At the moment, everything around her seemed unreal.

"I'll go meet the cops and lead them over here," Daisy said before starting off into the woods.

Cassie watched her leave, still dazed.

This hollow sensation was not at all what Cassie had expected to feel when she finally learned the truth about Jake's murder. In the end, finding out what had happened only led to more questions. The unanswerable ones about why people behaved the way they did. And about how she was supposed to go back to living a normal, everyday life knowing that Jake had died because of the stupid, petty ambitions of immoral, greedy people.

Daisy quickly returned with three cops who took custody of Al and Kirk Downing from Leon and Martin.

"Cassie."

In the midst of her emotional daze, Cassie heard Leon call her name. The care and concern in his voice felt more real than anything else in that moment. He wrapped his arms around her, held her close, until she finally gave in to the seemingly limitless tears she'd been holding on to for so long.

THIRTEEN

Late the next morning, Cassie sat in Sergeant Bergman's office at the Stone River Police Department feeling like she'd been run over by a truck. Between the physical fight with the first two gunmen before they'd taken her captive yesterday evening, the following chase through the forest, and the extreme emotional upheaval of the last few days, she'd had about all she could take.

Good thing she had Leon Bragg beside her, making her feel like she could withstand anything.

When he'd driven her back to the North Star Ranch last night, after giving his statement to local law enforcement officers and then changing the tire on his truck, he could have gone to his own home. The danger to Cassie, after all, had passed. But she'd asked him to remain at the ranch through at least another night and he'd agreed.

At the ranch, she'd explained everything that had happened in Rubyville to her dad, Sherry and Jay. After eating a turkey sandwich so that Sherry would stop worrying that she was in imminent danger of starving to death, Cassie had gone to bed. She'd expected to toss and turn all night while being tormented by bad dreams and traumatic memories. But that hadn't been the case. Instead, she'd slept well. Crying in the forest the night before must have been therapeutic.

Leon hadn't said a word about her tears soaking his shirt.

Right now they were waiting for Bergman to return from a meeting with the chief of police. Cassie hoped she would get some answers about Al and Kirk Downing. In particular, she wanted to make sure that Al's government connections as a soon-to-be-former mayor could not be used to help him or his son escape justice.

"You know, boss, you were a little slow running in the woods last night," Leon said to Cassie from the chair beside her, turning to face her, his brow furrowed. "Maybe you need to do some jogging and get back into shape."

Cassie raised her eyebrows and grinned in return. "Maybe *you* should lay off Sherry's desserts so *you* can run a little faster."

The man knew her well. He could tease her out of a funk whenever he wanted. And after four years of working so closely together, she knew him pretty well, too. They communicated by teasing, arguing, and talking about nearly everything other than their true feelings and relationship with one another. And *that* needed to change. She'd made that decision on the quiet drive home last night.

Bergman walked into his office carrying three large cups of coffee. "I know you two are tired and I figured this would help keep you awake." He set the cups on his desk and then handed one to Cassie and one to Leon.

"Thanks," Cassie said. While taking a sip, she noticed Bergman's wrinkled shirt and the beginnings of dark circles under his eyes. "Have you been working all night?"

The detective shrugged and took a sip of his coffee. "Who needs sleep?"

"Were you or the Montana cops able to get either of the Downing men to officially confess?" Leon asked, shifting his weight in his chair.

Bergman shook his head. "Neither of them is talking much, but we're getting a lot of information out of Seth Tatum. Seth and Kirk had been friends since they were in grade school, and Seth spent so much time hanging around the Downing household that he felt like family to them. So they talked freely in front of him. Al and Kirk assumed they had his loyalty. And they did—until they murdered Jake Hollister."

Bergman took a sip of coffee. "We don't have all the specific facts confirmed yet. This is a very complex case with a total of three murder charges, plus kidnapping and arson charges. The arrests last night happened over in Beckett County, Montana. But because the case includes the murder of an Idaho state trooper within the jurisdiction of Stone River, Idaho, Sheriff Grace Russell has allowed us to take the lead on the investigation and get first crack at pursuing charges against everyone involved."

"Will that include charges against Seth?" Cassie asked.

Bergman nodded. "Accessory to murder after the fact. He has to answer for his actions. But he'll probably make a deal with the prosecutor's office in return for all the information he's given us." He took another sip of coffee. "Seth told us where the gun used to kill Jake was tossed in to Lake Bell. At sunrise this morning, we had divers recover the weapon. It's already been matched with the slugs from the murder scene."

"Why were they so intent on killing Cassie?" Leon asked.

"It was because they were afraid she unknowingly had information that could get them locked up. You know about Jake stopping at the truck stop and recording images with his phone that apparently captured Kirk Downing in the middle of a drug deal. We uploaded all of Jake's digital files after his murder as a standard part of the investigation, but no one saw anything suspicious at the time. Knowing what we now know, we'll look again. But it's possible he was simply taking random video for some reason and never even focused on the images of Kirk Downing or Stefan Kasparov. He could have just picked the wrong time and place to shoot some video."

Cassie smiled softly to herself. "The forest comes right up to that parking lot. He might have seen a deer, or a hawk, or some other animal he wanted to take a picture of. He did that a lot."

Bergman nodded. "Unfortunately, Kirk knew Jake was a cop. He'd seen him just the day before when he'd joined his dad at city hall for a little meet-and-greet campaigning. Al was looking like a shoo-in for mayor. But he was running as a very law-and-order guy, so when Kirk admitted that he hadn't cleaned up his act as he'd promised his dad he would, and told him that he thought Jake might have pictures of him meeting with a drug supplier, Al was furious and panicked."

"But there was never any investigation into any of that," Cassie said.

"Yeah, they waited anxiously to see if anything

would happen. When nothing happened right away, Al figured that Jake hadn't recognized his son, but that he might eventually put things together once Al was elected mayor and pictures of his family were in the news. Al had plans to not only be mayor, but to use his insider information on property development plans and contracts out for bid. He'd make his friends Lee Ryder and Jim Ellison rich, as well as make himself wealthy by having them funnel some of that money back to him."

The detective paused to briefly look down at his coffee cup. "Eventually, their plan worked. But first, they had to get Jake out of the way. Lee Ryder had a job in the city hall building at the time, so he paid attention and, when he heard Jake in the building one day telling someone he was going to spend the upcoming Saturday morning fishing, Ryder told Al about it. Together they all decided that this would be their chance to silence Jake. And they did. The whole group was there when it happened. And because Seth had followed Kirk around like a shadow for so long, no one really worried about him, and he ended up in the middle of it.

"Seth left town shortly afterward," he continued. "For five years, it looked like Al and his son and their buddies were home free. But when Seth came to town for a friend's wedding, got arrested for driving under the influence and ran his mouth off to his cellmate, your informant, Phil Warner, the cold case warmed up again. Connie Ellison, the wife of the Downings' accomplice Jim Ellison, worked in the administrative office at the city jail. She overheard Cassie trying to determine the identity of someone who'd been in lockup and claiming to know something about the murder of a local Idaho state trooper. Connie alerted her husband because she had suspicions that he might have been mixed up in it. That's how the mayor and everyone else involved became aware that the cold case murder was heating up."

He turned to Cassie. "Al worried that the incriminating images of his son could have been stored in the cloud and that you might have access to that account and would eventually see them and put the story together. After the initial attack on the bridge failed, and you renewed your search for Jake's killer, he knew he needed to put on a show of helping you while trying to get you killed."

"So, Lee Ryder and Jim Ellison were the original shooters in the woods?" Leon asked.

Bergman nodded. "According to Connie, Al reminded them that if he went down for Jake's murder, they would, too. And since they were both avid outdoorsmen, they seemed to be the best assassins when it came time to kill you. After the original attack on the bridge didn't work, they tried to kidnap you. They were also the people who threw the explosives into the office and who ambushed you on the mountain pass."

"How exactly were they able to target us on the mountain pass?" Cassie asked.

"When Ryder and Ellison went to Saddleback looking for Seth to permanently shut him up after his drunken confession in the jail cell, they met his coworker Buzz and offered him big money for any information he could get them about Seth. That included a bonus to be paid later if they actually found him."

"So Buzz sold him out?" Cassie asked.

Bergman nodded. "Buzz says he had no idea there would be murder involved and that he thought the people looking for Tatum were all bill collectors. That's why he's stepped forward to help us now with the investigation."

The sergeant rubbed a hand over his jaw before continuing. "After Leon questioned him at the furniture store, Buzz called Ellison to tell him about it." Bergman settled his gaze on Cassie. "Ellison offered Buzz a lot of money if he'd tell his boss he was sick and quickly leave work to follow Leon. He had Buzz send him pictures, and Ellison could see that you were with Leon and that the both of you were traveling with Martin and Daisy in a second truck."

The detective leaned back in his chair. "Ellison left Idaho, headed for Montana to take advantage of the opportunity to kill you. We believe Ellison dropped off his partner, Lee Ryder, on the pass on his way to Montana before meeting with Buzz outside the restaurant where you ate dinner. He knew you'd drive through the pass at some point to get back home. Ryder climbed the ridge and got into firing position. Later, Ellison followed you back to Stone River. When you neared the spot where Ryder was situated atop the ridge, Ellison dropped back to keep himself out of danger and directed Ryder to open fire on Leon's truck. The intention was to shoot you or cause a fatal wreck."

"How did they find us in the ghost town?" Leon asked.

"Buzz was involved with that, as well. He says that after thinking about it, he remembered that while Seth wasn't a particularly outdoorsy guy, he liked history and enjoyed looking around and searching for old glass in Rubyville. So he wouldn't be surprised if Seth was hiding out either in the ghost town itself or at the campground near there. He called Ellison to tell him his thoughts. We believe that immediately after that, Ellison called Al to let him know that he and Ryder were headed to the area to search for Seth.

"We also believe Al and Kirk Downing then went to Rubyville with the intention of killing Seth and their accomplices, Ryder and Ellison. They probably figured they'd have an opportunity to kill you sometime in the future and then they'd be home free. It's possible the Downings didn't even know you were in Rubyville until Ryder and Ellison saw you there and let them know just before the mayor and his son arrived."

"So the gunshots we heard from behind the boardinghouse were Al and Kirk shooting it out with Ryder and Ellison?" Cassie asked.

"That's what it looks like."

"Bergman!"

Cassie glanced over her shoulder to see another detective standing several feet outside the office, gesturing at the door of a conference room.

Bergman downed the last of his coffee and stood. "I've got to go," he said. "We'll be in touch with you." He reached out to lightly squeeze Cassie's shoulder as he walked by.

After years of feeling like the edges of her life were frayed and coming undone, Cassie was looking forward to getting everything cleanly tied up. But she wasn't quite there yet.

Cassie tipped her head back to let the sun shine on her face as she sat in a bistro chair at a table she shared with Leon. They were seated on the sidewalk outside the café at the Bellport Inn near the park on the edge of Lake Bell. It felt good to be out in the open and not have to worry that someone would take a shot at her.

She and Leon had walked from the police station directly to the café since they'd both had only coffee for breakfast and were now famished.

"It's over," Cassie said, taking another couple of seconds to enjoy the sun on her face before tilting her head down and opening her eyes to look at Leon.

So much that had fueled the flames of stress in her life was now finally over. Her worry that her family or friends might be caught in the crossfire as someone tried to kill her was gone. So was the burdensome, heightened worry for her own safety. The worry that her business would fall apart because she was too busy trying to identify and capture the bad guys had vanished. And the worry that she was stuck, frozen in time, obsessed with solving the murder of her husband, was finally set free.

She'd been holding on to the idea of finding justice for Jake pretty tightly. Now, finally, she could turn that responsibility over to the justice system and truly let it go.

Most important, she could finally turn the bigger questions over to God and accept that He was in control of it all. As unfathomable as that might seem.

"Thank You, Lord," she said softly.

"Amen," Leon agreed.

A smile, warm and fuzzy and ridiculous, formed on her lips. An expression of what she felt in her heart. This man seated across from her knew her. She had no doubt that without her even explaining it, he knew what she was thankful for.

One of those things was, in fact, Leon. She kept her

gaze and her smile trained on him. He started to get a little fidgety, which was fun to watch. And if she didn't know better, she'd think a little bit of pink had appeared in those tanned, slightly weathered cheeks of his.

His hand was on the table, his finger and thumb resting on the handle of his coffee mug. She reached out and placed her hand atop his. Kept it there. And it kind of looked like Leon stopped breathing. She couldn't help but enjoy the little sense of power it gave her.

After a few seconds, he started to breathe normally again. He stopped fidgeting and returned her gaze. Held it.

Now it was Cassie's turn to feel a nervous flutter in her belly. She found herself taking shallow breaths. And then she saw the corner of Leon's mouth lift in a slight smile.

He'd taken control of the situation and flipped it on her.

Well, of course, he had. Leon Bragg was the best bounty hunter she'd ever worked with, and he was adept at taking control of a situation to make it go the way he wanted it to.

Well, two could play at that game.

The waiter brought their bill and Leon insisted on paying.

After the check was settled, they walked around the corner and headed up the street toward the Rock Solid Bail Bonds office. Repairs were in full swing. She'd put Harry in charge of overseeing everything since he'd had some construction experience.

"I know Jake will always have a place in your heart," Leon said as they walked. "But maybe now that so many questions have been answered and justice is being served, you might find it easier to move forward with your life. You said that was something you wanted to do."

"Did you mean move forward with *you*?" she asked, turning to give him her sauciest grin. "Was that a hint?"

He returned her grin, but then his expression slowly changed, like a serious realization was settling over him. Cassie had seen it before. And she knew what was coming. He was about to put some emotional distance between the two of them.

"I hope you find the right man one day," he said a little later, when they were almost at the Rock Solid Bail Bonds office.

She came to a halt. "What if the right man is you?"

He stopped beside her on the sidewalk and made a slight scoffing sound. "I've spent more than half my life living like the bail jumpers we chase. I couldn't ever be a cop because of my police record. I know I don't look like a nice guy because it's not that unusual to see people cross the street when they spot me coming down the sidewalk toward them." He sighed deeply. "I'm no Jake."

"Who said I was looking for a carbon copy of Jake?" Cassie demanded, frustration making her voice rise in volume. "After all the time we've spent working side by side, and everything we've been through together, how can you not know I value you exactly as you are?"

He stared. Apparently unable to open his mouth and *talk*.

Was he really going to make her plainly state her feelings first? Okay, fine.

"You're fired," she said.

He blinked. *"What?"*

"You heard me. And now that you're no longer my employee, I can tell you how I feel."

Before she could say anything further, Leon pulled her close and kissed her.

The satiny warmth of his lips pressed against hers felt even better than she'd imagined. He wrapped his arms around the small of her back, pulling her closer while still pressing his lips to hers. He took his time and, after he finally broke off the kiss, he nuzzled the side of her face. His warm breath trailed down the side of her neck, curling toward her collarbone.

It was a good thing he continued to hold her up, because she felt a little light-headed.

Slowly, she returned to her senses and realized that the man had managed to express his true feelings first. He'd flipped the situation on her *again.*

"I love you, Cassie," he said, his voice a low rumble near her ear. "I have loved you for a very long time."

"I can't tell you exactly when I started loving you," she said. "But I can tell you I'm never going to stop."

Leon dropped to his knee on the sidewalk and reached for her hand. "Cassie, will you marry me?"

She already knew what she needed to know about him. There really was no point in waiting and fiddling around with dating. "Yes, Leon, I will marry you. And the sooner we become husband and wife, the sooner I can hire you back. Because I have a strict policy about—"

The next thing she knew he was back on his feet and kissing her again. She vaguely heard Harry outside the office just a few feet away whooping and hollering, but the sound quickly faded. Like everything else faded away in the moment except for Leon and herself. Ready to move forward in life together.

EPILOGUE

One month later

Cassie and Leon were standing near a table loaded with fruit punch when Duke moseyed by, wagging his tail and knocking over nearly all of the filled cups. The big dog immediately lowered his head, guilty expression in his sweet brown eyes, obviously thinking he was in trouble.

Leon reached the dog first, scratched him behind the ears and told him it was okay, that he was still a good boy. Then he got the Great Dane mix to move a few feet away while Sherry righted the table and Daisy's friend and former boss, Millie, picked the cups up off the grass.

Cassie smiled at the sight of Leon, dressed in a nice suit and looking quite sharp, petting the dog and trying to make the animal feel better. Of course, little Tinker had to get in on the action and get a few pets, too. Leon Bragg might look like ten miles of rough road, but he'd managed to combine his tough past with God's grace until he'd been polished into a diamond. At least that's how Cassie saw her new husband as she looked at him right now. He was a diamond.

They were on the lawn in front of the house at North Star Ranch, taking a few minutes to relax and soak up the joy of their big day. The wedding ceremony had taken place at ten o'clock in the morning at the little country church Cassie's family had always attended. Since space had been limited, only close friends and family had attended. Leon had invited the uncle he was close to, along with ten family members who generally didn't have much to do with him, to the ceremony. He'd told Cassie that he hadn't expected any of them other than the uncle to show up. But four of his relatives had come. Seeing the look in Leon's eyes when he'd spotted them had been the best wedding present Cassie could have gotten.

The reception at the ranch was the event where they'd been able to let loose and invite everyone they could think of. It was an informal affair. Just a big barbecue with lots of burgers and ribs and roasted corn on the cob.

And there was pie. When Harry and Ramona Orlansky had gotten married, they'd decided to serve pie at the reception instead of wedding cake. The pies, baked by Ramona's parents, were so delicious that Martin and Daisy Silverdeer had chosen to serve pie at their reception, too. When it came to their turn, Cassie and Leon had stuck with Rock Solid bounty hunter tradition and served pie, as well. Because everybody loves pie.

It was now late in the afternoon. Guests were scattered across the property, some still seated at the banquet tables on the lawn, others were visiting the horses in the stables or just walking around North Star Ranch and enjoying a beautiful blue-sky Idaho day.

Tomorrow, Cassie and Leon would leave for Hawaii. It would be a new experience for both of them. And Cassie was all about having new experiences and forming new memories with her new husband.

"Duke! Tinker!" Cassie heard the sound of Adam calling the dogs. And, of course, the dogs took off running to find her father.

With his canine charges gone, Leon made his way back to Cassie. She couldn't help smiling as she gazed at that face she'd grown to love. At the man she loved.

"I'm just glad it was the dog that knocked everything over and not me." Leon reached for Cassie's hands. "Have I told you how beautiful you look?" he said. "How beautiful you *are*?"

"Only about thirty times today," she joked.

He stepped even closer to her. "Guess you'll have to get used to it. Because I need to make up for lost time."

"Oh, yeah?"

"Yeah." He gently squeezed her hands. "For years, I thought about how beautiful you were but I couldn't say it. I couldn't tell you that I loved you."

"In a way, I think I knew. And I obviously started feeling the same way about you."

He quirked an eyebrow. "You could have said something."

"Hey, be grateful for what you've got right now," she teased. She was certainly grateful for what she had.

He leaned in for a kiss. The weather was warm, but Cassie shivered nonetheless. It was a good shiver. Leon kept an arm wrapped around her shoulders, holding her close as they both turned to look across the ranch at their family and friends.

For Cassie, it felt good not to dwell on the past anymore.

She was happy to focus just on being right here, right now. Side by side with Leon. And that was exactly where the two of them wanted to be.

* * * * *

*If you enjoyed this Rock Solid Bounty Hunters
novel by Jenna Night, be sure to pick up
the other books in this miniseries.*

Fugitive Chase
Hostage Pursuit

Available now from Love Inspired Suspense!

Dear Reader,

Well, Cassie and Leon are on their way to Hawaii for their honeymoon. And things are relatively peaceful at North Star Ranch and in Stone River, Idaho. At least, for now.

In each of the Rock Solid Bounty Hunters' stories, at least one person has had to loosen their grip on the past a little so that they could move forward with their life. Examining your recollection of a difficult past experience so that you can consider it with a more healing perspective is not easy to do. Updating your self-image to reflect the person you are today isn't always so simple, either. Those are just a couple of examples of times when we need to press into God's grace to help us keep going.

I hope you've enjoyed your time in Stone River. I invite you to visit my website, JennaNight.com, where you can sign up for my mailing list and I'll keep you up to date on new book releases and show you book covers as soon as I get the green light to make them public. You can also keep up with me on my Jenna Night Facebook page or get alerts about upcoming books by following me on BookBub. My email address is Jenna@JennaNight.com. Feel free to drop me a line.

Kind regards,
Jenna